SHADOWRISE

SHADOWS OF THE VOID BOOK 4

J.J. GREEN

INFINITEBOOK

BOOK ORDER

The Books of Shadows of the Void - Complete Series

Prequel: Starbound
Book 1: Generation
Book 2: Stranded
Book 3: Dawn
Book 4: Shadowrise
Book 5: Underworld
Book 6: Burned
Book 7: Trapped
Book 8: Mars Born
Book 9: Shadow Battle
Book 10: Shadow War
Books 1 - 3 The Galathea Chronicles
Books 4 - 7 The Earth Chronicles
Books 8 - 10 The Galactic Chronicles

1

———

Lifting his duffle bag onto his shoulder, Carl Lingiari took a final look at his cabin before preparing to disembark the *Galathea*. He wasn't usually so sentimental, but the prospecting mission he'd just finished had been eventful. Hostile aliens called Shadows had killed the ship's officers and appeared as perfect copies of their victims, and Carl had fought alongside Harrington, the chief security officer, to save the ship. The menace of the Shadows had followed them to the colony planet, Dawn, which was supposed to have been free of the hostile aliens. It had turned out to be anything but.

The original pilot of the *Galathea* had been among the fatal casualties of the alien attack. For Carl, this meant that he'd gained precious flight hours piloting a starship, though it was the worst way for the opportunity to occur. He intended to put the experience to good use. He would pay his folks at home in Australia a brief visit, then he would apply for a full pilot's position and go touring the stars again.

"You all right in there, mate?" He directed the question

to his duffle bag. A pair of bright eyes peeked through the half-open zip.

"Yeah, but get a move on," Carl's friend, Flux, replied. "It's stuffy in here. And your socks smell. Have you washed them?" An alien resembling a cross between a sugar glider and a bat, Flux was hiding, ready for the disembarkation inspection. Pets were banned aboard ship—not that Flux considered himself a pet—and prospecting crews weren't allowed to bring anything back that they hadn't taken with them when they departed Earth territory, especially not any alien life forms.

Strictly speaking, this meant Flux should have been safe from confiscation because Carl had smuggled him aboard when they'd set off, but the higher-ups in Deep Space Customs wouldn't see it that way. Flux would have to hide, and Carl would employ a special signal an old girlfriend who worked in Customs had taught him. The signal would guarantee that his bag wouldn't be inspected.

His door chime sounded. Harrington was waiting outside, looking stormy.

"What's up?" asked Carl as he left his cabin and closed the door for the final time.

"Haven't you received Haggardy's message yet?" Harrington replied. "Check your interface."

Carl unzipped his bag, lifted a disgruntled Flux off of his screen, and pulled it out. The alert light was flashing, indicating a message had arrived. Flux must have been sitting on the speaker when it beeped.

Haggardy had taken over as the *Galathea's* master when Akabe Loba had died, and had avoided as much responsibility as was possible in his new position. Carl wondered what the man had to say now that was suddenly so important.

Harrington supplied the answer before he could even open the message.

"He wants us to lie about what happened," she said. "He's sent us a 'report' to repeat to the investigators so he doesn't get into trouble for not helping to save the officers from the Shadows. Kratting misborn. I'm damned well not lying for him."

"Crew to departure hatch," came a voice over the comm system. "Prepare to disembark."

Carl and Harrington set off, joining the crowds of shipmates heading in the same direction.

Carl wasn't surprised that Haggardy wanted to cover up his role in the events of the last few weeks. If Polestar or the Global Government found out the extent of his inaction, he would be dismissed and his pension withdrawn at the very least. At worst, he could be charged with criminal negligence and involuntary manslaughter.

"Does he really think he can brush everything under the carpet that easily?" Carl asked. "There's gotta be security vids of it all, and he can't expect the whole crew to lie for him."

"He doesn't need *everyone* to lie. The rest of the crew don't know what actually happened. All they saw was a bunch of officers fighting. They only had our word for it that the officers were alien imposters, and I'm sure some of them didn't believe us.

If we told the investigators Haggardy's side of the story, they'd buy it, I think. But there's no way in hell I'm lying for him."

"We don't have to lie," said Carl. He thumbed the interface screen. "If he's telling us we have to stick to his report, we've got the evidence right here." The screen brightened with the acting master's message.

"He isn't that dumb, Lingiari."

Carl scanned the writing for a moment. "Yeah, I see what you mean." Haggardy's report on the incident on K. 67092d was addressed to Carl, Harrington, and Sayen Lee. Navigator Lee had been seriously injured when the *Galathea* had crash-landed. Carl had heard she was at that moment being transferred from the ship's stasis room to the nearest genetic hospital, where doctors could assess the extent of her brain damage and grow her a clone if necessary.

The subject line of the message simply read FYI. Only the people addressed in Haggardy's message would understand its true meaning: that was the story, and they were expected to stick to it, or else...what?

"You aren't considering covering up for him, are you?" asked Harrington.

"No, 'course not," replied Carl, but he wondered what Haggardy would do when they didn't. The man had decades of service under his belt, and he probably had stacks of influential friends.

"Do you think they're going to use the same tests for Shadows that they had on Dawn?" asked Harrington. "Krat, I hope not. I mean, they say the testing's foolproof, and that a Shadow must have got onto Dawn another way, but I don't see how they can be so sure. I'd swear we brought one with us."

"What I don't get is, if they could test us here on Earth, why did they send us all the way to Dawn?" Carl said. "Unless the problem's bigger than we thought and they can't process everyone who arrives here? Anyway, we'll have to go along with it. They seem to think they know what they're doing, and it's out of our hands now. The only alternatives are to refuse us permission to disembark or to go right ahead and destroy the ship. That'd reduce the risk all right."

"Urgh, don't say that," said Harrington.

"Anyway, let's collect Makey on our way out. We can show him where to go and vouch for him while he claims refugee status."

"Good idea," Harrington replied.

"By the way, what's happening with the Paths?"

"They've been transferred to a quarantine ship. None of the xenobiologists seem to have heard of them. It'll be a while before they're cleared to go planetside. And Karrev and the others were taken down by police transport this morning. They've all been charged with mutiny."

When they reached Makey's cabin, they found the Dawn native cleaning the shower room, which was already spotless.

"Hey, mate, you don't need to do that," said Carl. "They're gonna go through this ship and sterilize it top to bottom once everyone's off. Come on, we've got to disembark. We've got heaps of testing to get through once we're planetside."

The skinny young man straightened up and put down a face cloth he'd been using to wipe the surfaces. "If you're sure. I don't want to seem ungrateful for the cabin and free passage to Earth."

"No one thinks you're ungrateful for the chance to come with us," said Harrington. "I just wish Haggardy had agreed to bring some of Dawn's inhabitants."

"Me too," said Makey. "I'll get my stuff."

As the kid quickly packed his bag, Carl wondered what he would think of Earth. It was very different from the poor farming community he'd left behind. The kid would see luxuries and lifestyles that he'd probably never dreamed of, and a big gap between those who could and couldn't afford them.

The three joined the stragglers leaving the ship to board the shuttle that would take them to a spaceport in London, UK. From there, they could catch shuttles that would take them to the other side of the planet within a few hours, or airplanes that would get them to their destination much slower, but much cheaper.

At the departure hatch, a ginger-haired woman—the engineer-in-training MacAdam—was waiting for them. She was smiling like all her birthdays had come at once.

"You haven't disembarked yet?" asked Harrington.

"No, not yet," MacAdam replied. "I wanted to take this last chance to thank you. I might not see you again once we all go our separate ways."

"How come? You hanging up your wrench?" Carl asked. Prospecting crews often encountered old shipmates in the course of their work.

"I might be." The engineer grinned. "I sent a request to visit my kids, and I just heard that I've got an appointment. If I manage to stay clean for another six months, they said I stand a good chance of getting them back."

"Great news," said Carl. He had a feeling that Harrington's mail to the relevant authorities about MacAdam turning over a new leaf might have had something to do with the favorable response to her request.

"Yeah, great news," Harrington said, followed by, "Krat."

Haggardy was striding toward them. They'd nearly made it onto the shuttle without meeting the brown-noser.

"Lingiari, Harrington, just the people I wanted to see. MacAdam, and..." The acting master's eyebrows rose. "I remember you," he spluttered as he recognized Makey. "I gave instructions that you were *not* to board the ship."

"Not a lot you can do about it now, is there?" said Carl.

"Makey, wait for us when you're through the testing. We'll point you to the refugee office."

As the kid went away, Haggardy followed him with his gaze, then turned his narrowed eyes to Carl and Harrington. MacAdam made herself scarce, mouthing 'goodbye'.

Haggardy said, "I gave explicit instructions—"

"What's done is done," said Harrington. "The kid's here now, and he can claim refugee status. It's going to be a long afternoon, so we'll be on our way."

"No you don't," Haggardy said. "Until you leave the ship, you two are still under my command, and I *order* you to remain. I have something to tell you."

Folding his arms over his chest, Carl waited with the grim-faced Harrington.

After checking that the rest of the crew were out of hearing range, Haggardy said, "I sent you both a report detailing what happened when we first encountered the Shadows. You are to memorize and repeat the facts as I stated them. There is to be no mention of your versions of the events, no interpretations, twisting, or embellishments of the truth as I have laid it out. Is that clear?"

"No way, Haggardy," Harrington said through her teeth. "No way am I lying for you. Forget it."

"Yeah," said Carl, "that's not happening, mate. You didn't do your job. That's the truth, and that's what I'm telling anyone who asks. Let's go," he added to Harrington.

The two walked away, and Haggardy shouted after them, "If you know what's good for you, you'll tell *my* truth. Or I'll make things very difficult for you. Very difficult indeed."

As they went through the exit hatch and boarded the shuttle, Carl wondered what Haggardy meant.

2

——————

By the time Carl had passed through the Shadow testing and then Customs, it was late evening. He stepped out of the spaceport and into the heat, humidity, noise, and bright lights of London. Flux had long ago fallen asleep in his bag. When Carl checked on him, the animal's closed eyes and half-open mouth with its double row of needle-sharp teeth showed through the transparent wings he'd wrapped over his face.

Carl yawned. He had an appointment the next day with Polestar's investigators. He needed to find somewhere to stay the night.

Even at that hour, the multi-lane road that skirted the spaceport was busy with traffic, both at street level and just above as cars passed slower-moving vehicles by flying briefly over them. Carl wondered how long it would be before constant hover-driving was legal, and the traffic would split into road- and just-above-road level, and after that, maybe a third level? He didn't spend enough time on Earth to bother with buying a hovercar of his own, and driving had become all computer-automated, which took the fun out of it. He would have liked to drive/fly, dodging up and down and around the other cars.

He felt a tug on his sleeve. A dero had appeared beside him, unnoticed while Carl was watching the traffic. The man was barefoot, and from his overgrown toenails to his matted hair, he was grimy. A nauseating smell infiltrated Carl's nostrils.

"Just off a prospector, ain't ya?" the dero said. "You must be rolling in creds. I used to work the prospectors, too, till I caught thermatic plague. They cured me, but I'll never work again. Not like you. You look like a healthy bloke. Got years in you. Spare us some cred, eh?" The man was cradling a reader. The machine was old and cracked, but the display still glowed.

Carl didn't believe the man's story. No one survived thermatic plague. The dero probably lived from one run to the next. Carl didn't like the idea of supplying the man's habit, but for some, that was as much as their lives would ever hold.

"All right, give it to me," he said, taking the ancient reader from the man. He pressed the credchip embedded in his wrist to the scanner before typing in a nominal amount. When it registered the deduction from his account, he returned the reader.

The dero squinted at the display. "That's all you're giving me?" he said.

"Hey, if you don't want it..." Carl held out his hand to take the reader back, but the man clutched it to his chest and shuffled off without looking back.

"Thanks," Carl called out after him. He was beginning to remember why he spent so much of his time in deep space. The realization arrived quicker each time he touched down.

He yawned again. He needed to find a bed before he fell

asleep on his feet. After checking on Flux a second time, he zipped up his bag and headed toward the autocab station. He wished he had someone to carry him around in a bag while he slept.

At the station, no autocabs were available and, according to the screen, none were due to return for another half an hour. *Krat.* He sat on the bench and pulled out his personal interface. He'd handed over his ship's one to the investigators of the incidents on K. 67092d. He hoped they would let him leave in enough time to catch the shuttle to Sydney the next day. He didn't want to wake his folks up with his surprise arrival in the early hours of the morning.

He tried to contact another autocab service, but they were all busy. He would just have to wait for a spaceport autocab to return. He started to look up local hotels on his interface to book a room. He found a place that didn't look like too much of dive but wasn't too pricey either. He was about to pay for it when the bright lights of an autocab caught his attention. One had returned earlier than the system had predicted. It drew up in front of him.

As he got up, the door opened. Harrington was inside. She leaned over the seat and smiled at him.

"Can I give you a lift?"

Carl laughed, put his bag on the back seat carefully to avoid disturbing Flux, and got in.

"I thought I'd return your favor," Harrington said as the door closed and the vehicle moved away. "Though I'm not exactly saving your life."

She'd been referring to the time he'd picked her up in a shuttle when she was under attack on Dawn. He said, "Thanks, but you would've got yourself out of that scrape if I hadn't happened along."

"I don't think so."

"I appreciate it anyway. How'd you know I was waiting?"

"I was hanging about, just in case. I saw all the autocabs got taken fast. Thought you might need a ride."

"Thanks a lot. I'm going here." He showed her the hotel he'd picked.

"Hmmm...well..." Harrington gave him a sidelong look. "My place isn't far. How about you save some creds and stay with me tonight?"

"That'd be great." The evening was getting better and better.

After Carl's agreement, a slight awkwardness invaded the atmosphere in the autocab. He wasn't sure what Harrington's intentions were. Maybe she was only offering him a place to sleep, or maybe she had more in mind. He was confused about how she felt toward him, and his feelings about her weren't yet clear to him.

When he'd first known her, she'd been a crush of his, but the woman had been so wrapped up in doing her job, she'd barely seemed to register that he existed. Dealing with the Shadow officers aboard the *Galathea* had brought them closer together, and he'd felt like he was getting to know the inner Harrington a bit better.

But then she'd grown close to a lieutenant stationed on Dawn. He'd backed off, assuming that he'd imagined her increasing feelings toward him. After she'd killed the Shadow of the lieutenant, however, it had been *him* she'd turned to in her confusion and grief.

The truth was, he had no idea where he stood with her.

The autocab was turning off the street, and a wide garage door lifted up, revealing the entrance to an underground carpark. Carl leaned back as the vehicle's nose dipped and it went down into the dark space. The cab halted abruptly next to an elevator and the doors popped open.

"This is it," Harrington said. "Don't forget your stuff."

"You do live close to the spaceport."

The woman shrugged as they went into the elevator. "It's convenient. I usually signup again pretty quick after finishing a mission."

The conversation lapsed and the awkwardness continued as they went up thirty floors.

After getting off the elevator, Harrington pressed her wrist to the door scanner, and the door opened. "It's small, but I don't need much," she said as they went in.

She wasn't joking that it was small, Carl thought. He put down his bag. He'd heard that space was at a premium in London, but Harrington's apartment was so small it would have fitted into his parents' living room. The place reminded him of a starship cabin. The bed, kitchen, and living area were combined, and a single door led to the shower room. The place was clean and tidy, and it didn't look poor, but it had an institutional feel to it. Someone had told him once that Harrington had grown up in a government orphanage, and the gossip rang true now that he saw how she lived.

"Are you hungry?" asked Harrington. "We can order something."

"No, I'm not. How about you?"

"No." She sat on the bed.

"So...I'm pretty bushed," Carl said. "I'll take the couch."

"Oh, okay."

Did she sound disappointed?

"I'm going to freshen up," Harrington said. She went into the shower room.

Carl got Flux out of his bag. The creature remained sound asleep. He put him on the end of the couch and covered him with a throw. While waiting for Harrington to finish, he looked out of her window and across the cityscape. Rivers of light marked the roads and freeways. No stars were visible due to their glow.

At the nearby spaceport, a shuttle was arriving from a starship, and Carl squinted in its glare as it landed. When the engines had been shut off, he recognized it was the latest model. He'd never flown one, but that no longer mattered. His eyes were on higher stakes. He was looking forward to his first starship commission.

Behind him, the door to the shower room opened, and Harrington appeared. She'd changed into loose pajamas and her hair was damp and messy from towel drying. Her sleepwear was typical Harrington—more functional than feminine—yet his long-time attraction to her remained the same.

"Your turn," she said.

He went into the shower room and mulled over what he should do as he got ready for bed. He was confused. Should he make a move? Was that why she'd brought him home? Or was she only doing a shipmate a favor? Harrington wasn't the flirtatious type. He found her hard to read.

If he tried something and the timing wasn't right, he might kill any chance he had of getting closer to her. He recalled again how shaken up she'd been by killing the Shadow of the soldier she'd got close to on Dawn. That decided it. He would wait for a crystal-clear signal before he would try to take things any further. She had to still be pretty upset by that incident.

Carl returned to the living room. Harrington was already

in bed. They said goodnight, and after she'd turned out the light and dimmed the window to near darkness, he lay awake for a while, watching the faint trails of light from incoming and outgoing space shuttles shining through the glass. Memories of their encounters with Shadows played in his mind, as well as thoughts about the possible repercussions of the upcoming investigation. Concerns about Haggardy's possible methods for getting revenge also nagged at him.

From the sound of her breathing, he could tell Harrington was still awake.

"Have you thought about what you're going to tell them at the investigation tomorrow?" he asked.

"No. What's to think about? I'll tell them what happened of course."

"Yeah, but...I've been thinking about what Haggardy said. Do you think he can really do something serious if we don't go along with his story?"

"I don't know. Does it matter?" Harrington asked.

"It matters to me. Flying's my life. I dunno what I'd do if he got my license revoked."

Harrington's soft sigh breathed out into the night. "We don't have a choice. We have to tell the truth, no matter what. Haggardy's a real misborn. We can't let him get away with it. It wouldn't be right. If he'd done something when I warned him about Loba, maybe none of those officers would have died."

"I'm not disagreeing, but what's done's done. And that was his last mission. He's retiring now. He's not a danger to anyone anymore."

"Krat, Lingiari," Harrington replied, her voice rising, "I can't believe you're even saying that. You were with me there on the *Galathea*, right? You did know all those officers too?"

"All right, calm down. I was just thinking out loud. Geez."

Harrington mumbled something inaudible, and her sheets rustled. She didn't speak again. After a while, her breathing became deep and regular as she fell asleep.

3

"Thank you for your time, Pilot Lingiari," said the chief investigator, extending his hand.

Carl sat up from his slouched position and reached to take the man's hand. He was in front of a team of five investigators, and he'd been there so long he'd lost track of time. "That's it? I can go?" His throat ached from answering the men and women's questions, and his head buzzed from going over the events on K. 67092d again and again.

The questioning had felt more like an interrogation than an investigation. He was glad he'd told them nothing but the truth according to his memory of the events. He would never have been able to keep track of Haggardy's lies if he'd decided to go along with the man's story.

"Yes, we have no more questions for you at the moment," said the investigator. He glanced at his colleagues on his right and left as he spoke. All of them shook their heads.

"Great." Carl stood and stretched.

"But, until the investigation is concluded, you are not to leave Earth," added the man.

"What?" Carl stopped mid-stretch and deflated a little. "How long's it gonna take? I mean, I'm a deep space pilot. I've gotta leave Earth to work."

"We understand. The investigation shouldn't take too long. I'm afraid I can't promise you anything more than that, however. We'll notify you when we reach our final conclusions."

"Great," Carl repeated with less enthusiasm. He took his jacket from the back of his chair and made his way out of the Global Security Headquarters. It was nighttime. He'd been answering questions the whole day. He checked the time and realized that he might make the last shuttle to Sydney if he hurried.

He requested an autocab on his interface and waited for it to arrive. It would be a close thing to make the shuttle flight, but after a day of talking about Shadows, fighting, and death, he had a strong urge to set eyes on his aging parents and his childhood home again.

The shuttle would be worth the extra expense to feel the hot Australian sun on his back again the next day. Outback New South Wales was worlds better than muggy, humid, polluted London.

He opened his bag. "We're going home, mate," he said to Flux, who was inside, eating a cracker.

"About bloody time," replied the creature. "I've been in this kratting bag nearly two days. I need to stretch my wings."

Flux wasn't the friendliest of aliens at the best of times, but he'd only had an hour or so of flying outside Harrington's window that morning, and the creature's grumpiness was only to be expected.

Carl jumped into the autocab that arrived, and he jumped out of it again at the spaceport. He ran through the terminal to make the shuttle, and soon he was strapped in and waiting to take off.

Night changed to dawn as he flew to Australia. The sun was coming up over Bondi when the shuttle touched down. Carl had managed a short nap on the flight, but his eyes were heavy and gritty by the time he hired a car at Sydney spaceport. He told the car the address of his parents' farm beyond the Blue Mountains and settled down to catch up on his sleep while it took him there.

As his eyes closed, he imagined his parents' surprise when he turned up months earlier than expected. His mum wouldn't have cooked his favorite meal, as had become a homecoming tradition since he'd first left home to go to flight school, but it didn't matter. He was smiling as he fell asleep imagining the happiness on his mum's face when she set eyes on him.

The pinging of the rental car door opening awakened him. On the adjoining seat, Flux had unzipped Carl's bag from the inside. His brown button nose poked out first, followed by black, beady eyes and large, tufted ears.

"Wake up, idiot, we're home," he said as he climbed out of the bag and spread his wings. "Ah, that's better," he said before jumping over Carl and through the open door. "I'm off to catch some breakfast. Say hi to your folks. I'll see you guys later." The alien flew off, gaining height to fly over the eucalypts that edged Carl's parents' farm.

Carl grabbed his bag and closed the car door. He would leave it in the road. The farm was in an area that saw little more than local traffic. He went toward the farmhouse, which stood at the end of a driveway. Though it was still early morning, he was a little surprised his folks hadn't come out to greet him. His mum and dad were usually up with the sun. Maybe they were already out in the yard or working in the fields.

He went up the driveway and around the back of the house. Only delivery drones used the front door. No one was in the yard. He tried the back door, but it was locked. Carl's hand dropped in surprise. The back door was never locked. He stepped backward and peered at the upper floors of the house. His parents' bedroom window glass was clear, which meant they were up.

Returning to the house, he looked in the downstairs windows, cupping his hands around his eyes. All the downstairs rooms at the back were empty, and in the kitchen there were no signs that breakfast had taken place. He knocked on the back door. No one answered. After three or four more tries, he went out into the yard again and shouted up, "Mum, Dad."

He ran around the house to the front, but that door was locked too.

Carl decided to investigate the barn. If his parents were out working in the fields, equipment would be missing. But when he checked, everything seemed to be in its place. He wondered if they could have gone for a walk around the farm. It was possible, but why would they lock the door?

A terrible fear rose in Carl. He tried to quell it with reasoning. He tried to tell himself that his parents might have gone away to visit a relative, or they might have had another reason for leaving their cherished farm, but he couldn't convince himself that something wasn't very wrong.

He needed some help. Carl tilted back his head, put his hands to his mouth and shouted, "Cooee." The sound echoed back from the farmhouse and surrounding trees. A few minutes later, Flux appeared over a wattle tree and glided down to land on Carl's head before hopping onto his shoulder.

"Something's up, right?" Flux asked.

"You noticed?" said Carl. "I was gonna ask if you'd seen Mum or Dad about the place."

"Nope. Haven't seen them anywhere, and what's more, look around you, mate."

Carl went up a low rise, and gazed at the fields, the yard, and the house. His alien friend was right. The farm looked as though no one had been there in weeks. In his concern over his missing parents, he hadn't noticed that the house windows were grimy with red dust—something his dad would never have tolerated—and that the yard was thick with dead leaves and other plant debris that had blown in from the fields.

And the fields themselves—where was that year's crop? The ground should have been filled with green shoots at that time of year, but it looked as though it hadn't even been sown. A hard crust covered the land. The soil hadn't been tilled since the previous season's harvest. How long had his parents been away?

Carl's legs felt weak. He sat down right there in the cobbled yard, fear gripping him. He took his interface from his bag, and with trembling fingers he called the nearest neighbor. Mrs. Jesson had been friends with his parents all his life. If anyone would know where they were it would be her.

The neighbor answered, and her voice became full of sorrow and concern the second she recognized Carl's voice.

"Oh, love, I'm sorry. I thought you might know where they are."

"What? Have they gone missing? How long has it been?"

"Come over, Carl, and I'll tell you everything I know. It isn't right to talk about it over the phone."

"All right. I'll be there in a minute."

Carl jogged the kilometer over the fields to the neighbor's house, dreading to hear what she had to say. She was standing at her open door, waiting for him.

"What's going on, Mrs. Jesson?" asked Carl as he wiped his feet on her doormat. Flux was perched on his shoulder. As Carl went inside, the creature took off and circled the room twice before settling on the top of a display cabinet holding the woman's prized blue heeler ornaments collection. Flux was never normally allowed inside Mrs. Jesson's home as he'd never quite embraced house training, but she must have felt the occasion warranted an exception.

"Carl, dear, please sit down. You really don't have any idea where Bernard and Joyce have gone? We searched high and low for them. We told the police, and we locked the place up so nothing got stolen. It was lucky they gave up raising horses. It looked like they'd been gone two or three days before anyone realized." Reading Carl's expression, the older woman began to weep. "I'm so sorry. You were our last hope."

"Mrs. Jesson, what's happened to my parents?"

"Dearie, I don't know how to tell you this. Your mum and dad have been missing for three months. The police sent a message to your company to pass on. Didn't it get through?"

4

____

When Sayen Lee woke up, she knew something was wrong. She tried to make sense of the feeling. Then, as always, the realization hit as her memory returned. She'd been injured in the crash-landing on K. 67092d, and now all that remained of her mind was trapped within a brain that no longer controlled her body. Machines were keeping her heart beating and her lungs breathing. She was in stasis, and though she could think, hear, and speak, she was otherwise entirely cut off from the world.

Except...except...Sayen could feel. She was lying on sheets, and air moved gently on her skin. Her heart began to race. A beeping sounded.

"She's coming around," said an unfamiliar voice.

"Sayen, oh, Sayen," said another voice. Her mama. It was her mother speaking. The events of the last few days came flooding back to her. Could she...move? Was it possible...? Sayen had grown so used to not being able to open her eyes that she had to make a conscious effort to do it. She willed her eyelids to lift. A blur of indistinguishable shapes and light came into her view.

Footsteps sounded beside her, moving away. A door opened. "Craven," her mother called. "Get in here. She's woken up. Our baby's awake."

The footsteps returned.

Sayen forced her lips and voice box to work. "M...mama?" Her voice was no more than a whisper.

"Oh, sweetheart." Her mother's voice broke. The door opened again. More footsteps sounded, heavier and firmer than her mother's.

"Sayen, darlin'," said her father, "now don't you try to move or say a thing. The nurse has called the doctor, and she'll be here any minute. It's a miracle, Carleen, a miracle."

The shapes Sayen saw were becoming more defined by the second. They were multi-colored tiles, lined with thin light strips. But the lights weren't on. Her vision was filled with sunlight. The sound of her mother's sniffles was coming from her right-hand side, and the window was to her left.

Sayen felt like crying herself. The operation had been a success. The genetics team had grown her a new body, and they'd taken all the knowledge, memories, and personality contained in her old brain and transferred it to the new one. She'd survived. She would move, eat, speak, live again.

After Dr. Sparks had told her about her accident, and that it would be a long time before the *Galathea* could return to Earth, if ever, she'd thought she was living a kind of half-death, and that her real demise was only delayed a little. It had been good, of course, to talk to Carl and Jas and others aboard the ship, and to help out with their problems, but she'd given up on any chance that she might be saved.

Yet here she was, in a brand new body. And not only was

it brand new, but it was also enhanced. She'd been fitted with the latest in organic-synthetic technology. She didn't only have a new body, she had a *better* one.

The door opened again. "Hi, Sayen. I'm Doctor Evans, and I'm in charge of your treatment. Do you remember me? We had a long talk before we attempted the transfer. Now, I don't want you to say a thing. Just close your eyes once for yes, twice for no, okay?

"So, how're you feeling, sugar? You feeling okay?"

Sayen closed her eyes once.

"Great. Do you have any pain anywhere?"

Sayen blinked twice.

"Even better. Well..." A shadow crossed Sayen's vision as the doctor moved past, blocking the sunlight. "All your vitals are looking great, honey. I don't like to be too optimistic— there's plenty that could go wrong even at this stage—but I think you're gonna be fine. Mr. and Mrs. Lee, could you join me outside, please?"

Her parents and the doctor left the room, but Sayen remembered one of her new enhancements. She strained her hearing hard, and through the closed door, she could clearly make out the conversation the doctor was having with her parents. Had the doctor under-estimated the quality of the hearing the cloning service had supplied, or did she intend for Sayen to hear what she said?

"Mr. and Mrs. Lee, I know I already told you this, but I wanted to emphasize that it's very, very early days with Sayen. She's got her new body, but you have to remember that she's spent quite a while trapped in her mind. It'll take her some time to get used to controlling her movements. She'll be like a little baby learning to walk. She'll learn faster than a child because she's done it before, but she will have to learn."

"I understand, Doctor," said her mother. "We're prepared to pay for the very best in therapy to get her back to normal."

"Yup," added her father. "Whatever it takes."

"I know you are. You've both been very generous, and we all appreciate your kind donation to the hospital. But the real reason I wanted to speak to you was so I can be totally sure you understand she might not have all the mental capabilities she once had. Even without the death of brain tissue, there's no guarantee we can recover *everything* from the old mind, and after Sayen's accident…"

"We do understand," came her father's deep voice.

"We know, Doctor, we know. But it doesn't matter. You brought our baby girl back, and we can never thank you enough…" Her mother began to weep again.

"Just doing our jobs, Mr. and Mrs. Lee," said the doctor, "but it's a pleasure. A real pleasure. Now, why don't you go spend some time with your daughter? Just an hour or so. Please continue to resist the urge to hold or touch her, however tempting I know that must be. Her body is very, very fresh. We were forced to push the envelope on getting her transferred into it, in consideration of the conditions she'd been stored in. If we'd waited any longer, well, let's just say it might have been a very different Sayen you would be taking home."

"We'll be careful," said her mother. "Don't you worry." She blew her nose. "We won't let anything bad happen to her ever again."

～

THREE DAYS LATER, Sayen could sit up, and she was eating, drinking, and speaking normally. She was still experiencing the sheer joy of being alive. She would spend hours looking out the window, studying every feature of the hospital's lavish garden. Each flower, plant, insect, and bird delighted her. She felt like she'd never truly appreciated how beautiful the world was until she'd been nearly taken from it.

The hospital was wonderful too. Everything was so clean. She couldn't have wished for a neater or more dirt- and germ-free room.

Her doctor had told her that the next day she could begin learning to walk, and that to pass the time, she was allowed to start having one or two visitors. She'd known exactly who she'd wanted to see and she'd made a couple of calls before pleading with her parents to take a break and have some time to themselves when her visitors arrived. Her real reason for asking them to leave her alone was so that they wouldn't overhear upsetting details about what had happened aboard the *Galathea*.

The next day, a face appeared at the small window in her door. Sayen grinned and waved Harrington into the room.

"You get sick in style," were the security officer's first words as she came in.

"Thanks for coming. I'm not sick. I'm here to get better."

Harrington perched on the edge of her bed, squashing the mattress.

"Is Lingiari coming too?" she asked Sayen.

"No, I can't contact him."

"Must be busy with his parents." The woman studied her. "You look...totally the same."

Sayen laughed. "What were you expecting?"

"I don't know. I thought you could choose what you wanted for your new body? Like, height, size, shape, hair, eye, and skin color. Everything."

"I suppose I could have, but I didn't want to. I just asked for a clone. Are you saying there's something wrong with how I look?" She laughed again. "Seriously, why change anything? I like the way I am. And so do my parents. They've gotten used to the old Sayen. If I looked any different, it would be weird."

"I guess so," said Harrington. "But...are you sure you wouldn't rather be a little taller?"

The security officer maintained a deadpan expression long enough for Sayen to begin to look outraged, then both women burst into giggles.

As their laughter subsided, Sayen said, "I'm not totally the same, you know."

"Really? What's different?"

"Well, for one thing...I, er...I know, I'll show you. Let's arm wrestle."

"Sure," said Harrington, her eyebrows rising. She pushed her sleeve up to her elbow and rested it on the bed tray. Sayen did the same and grabbed the woman's hand. In a matter of moments, Harrington's forearm was flat against the tray.

"Woah," she said. "Let's try again. Maybe you caught me by surprise."

Harrington lasted a few moments longer the second time, but the victory was just as decisive.

"That's amazing. Is it just your arms that are stronger, or are you like that all over?"

"My muscles are enhanced with synthetic fibers," Sayen said. "And that's not all." She paused dramatically.

"Go on, tell me what else you've had done."

"Enhanced hearing *and* sight. And my skin can withstand freezing and boiling temperatures."

"Wow, that's impressive. It sounds like you didn't come too badly out of nearly dying."

"Huh, yeah, well, I'd rather that hadn't happened, but I'm not complaining about the end result. Though I think my parents' accountant might be. You know, Jas, I used to be so afraid of everything. I wouldn't even set foot on an alien planet."

"I remember."

"Something's changed in me. When I came so close to dying, I realized I'd never really lived. Do you know what I mean?"

"I guess so."

"After I get my strength back, I'm not going to hide away anymore. I'm going to take risks. I'm going to live my life to the full, even if it means a little danger now and then."

"That's great. I'm happy for you. Just...take things easy at first, okay?"

"Of course I will. But what's been happening? What are the results of the investigation? Have they arrested Haggardy yet?"

"No, not yet. I told them everything that happened, and they said they'd let me know the verdict, but I haven't heard anything so far, and there's been nothing on the news. I wish they'd hurry up. I just want to move on, you know? It's been longer than a week. I'm ready to sign up for another mission."

5

———

J as couldn't believe it. She was at home in her apartment, and she'd been standing when the message appeared on her interface, but her knees buckled and she sat on her bed as she read it.

All individuals involved in the attempted capture by unknown aliens of the prospecting starship Galathea while it was in orbit around K. 67092d are found to be innocent of any dereliction of duty or other criminal or civil culpability in the resultant loss of life. No legal wrongdoing on behalf of any Polestar employees involved, living or dead, has been found.

How could it be true? She'd told them all of it, beginning to end, and her story would have been totally different from Haggardy's. The investigation committee *must* have known one of them had to be lying. How could they have found no one guilty? Didn't they even suspect that something wasn't right? People had died. Margret Statton and nineteen officers had lost their lives. Even Loba deserved some kind of justice for his death. Haggardy shouldn't be able to get away with his cowardly and negligent behavior.

After staring at the screen for several more moments,

and resisting the urge to throw the interface across the room, Jas released a groan of frustration. She would never, never understand the workings of governments, or human beings in general.

She got up and went to her window. Looking out across the spaceport, she went over the events of the last few days. It looked like the investigation into the events with the Shadows was over, and despite what she'd thought was a growing closeness with Lingiari after what had happened with the Shadows on Dawn, he didn't seem that interested in her.

She'd messaged him once or twice, but she hadn't received a reply. She suspected that now that Sayen was better, the two of them would get together. The pilot had spent a lot of time with her while she was in stasis. She wished the couple well, but she couldn't help but feel a little sad. The more she'd gotten to know the pilot, the more she'd liked him, even though he'd wavered over telling the truth about Haggardy. She understood how important his job was to him. Her career was important to her too.

A shuttle was taking off. Her gaze followed its glowing path into the hazy blue sky. Somewhere up there, out of sight, a space vessel awaited its passengers. Maybe it was a prospector like the *Galathea*, or a transport to Mars, Europa, Titan, Callisto, or Ganymede, or maybe it was an alien vessel belonging to one of the Transgalactic Council allies.

Jas's heart yearned for the simplicity of space, far from the complex and bewildering machinations of humankind. It was time for her to return to the stars and her job working with the predictable, comprehensible defense units. She knew it was crazy, but she liked the fighting androids better than some people she knew. She'd even said goodbye to them before disembarking the *Galathea*. They hadn't replied, but she'd felt like they were a little bit sorry to be parted from her too. It had probably been her imagination.

Scouting for danger, protecting, and defending—these were concepts she could wrap her head around, even though they weren't easy in practice. Still, she could understand them. Yes, it was time to get back to work.

She reached for her interface and searched for current deep space security job openings, filtering the results for prospecting ships leaving within the next week. She didn't anticipate too many problems finding another berth. Her qualifications and experience counted heavily in her favor. Most people in her line of work switched to another profession within their first few years, assuming they survived. And she wasn't fussy about pay. Her bank account was already stacked with more creds than she would ever spend. A life in government institutions had left her uncomfortable with frivolity and luxury.

Five positions popped up on the screen. One was a two-year mission to a far-distant, little-explored section of the galaxy. It was another Polestar job. They weren't the best employers, but they weren't the worst either. Jas applied. With luck, she would be off the planet the day after tomorrow.

She composed a final mail to Lingiari, telling him she'd enjoyed working with him and wishing him well. Next, she wrote to Sayen and told her she hoped her recovery was going well, and that maybe they might meet on a starship somewhere if the navigator decided to return to work. From what she'd understood as the cost of Lee's treatment, it looked like she didn't have to worry about never working again.

Getting up, Jas went to put on a light jacket. She wanted to head out for a final meal at a local noodle shop before she embarked on another mission. Her favorite restaurants were about the only thing she missed of Earth.

Her interface pinged. Had Lingiari finally replied? She checked the screen. No. It was a mail from Polestar. Thinking the reply was suspiciously quick, she opened it. The position had been filled. *Krat.* She would have to apply for the shorter missions. They were all pretty much the same—one-year trips to planets that had been passed over in the first prospecting rush. Usually, this was because they were too high or low gravity, or had some other feature that made the potential profits from resource extraction marginal.

Whatever. A longer assignment would have been better, but Jas didn't really mind what kind of planets she worked on. She applied to all four positions, put on her jacket and went out.

In the basement of a department store, she went to one of the many small restaurants that lined the walls. She took a seat and spoke her request into the ordering mic. As always, her height and coloring made her stand out. The rest of the patrons in the basic restaurant watched her for a few moments before returning to their meals. She didn't have to wait long before a bowl of noodles appeared on a serving cart and trundled over to her.

She'd barely begun eating before her interface pinged again, twice, in her pocket. She took it out and propped it up against the condiment containers on the table. She'd received two mails replying to her job applications. That was fast. She opened the messages and read that both positions were no longer open. Her stomach began to sink. Three jobs filled as soon as she applied for them? It was too much of a coincidence.

With a sense of foreboding, she continued to eat. Sure

enough, a few minutes later, a third mail arrived. The company was very sorry, but her application had been unsuccessful. *Krat. Krat. Krat.* She'd finished her meal, paid, and was leaving the restaurant when the fourth mail arrived. She almost didn't bother opening it. The security officer position had been posted in error, the message said, and the company was not accepting applications.

It had to be Haggardy's doing. He hadn't only got off scot-free, he'd called on all the contacts he'd built up over his long career and managed to get her blacklisted. *Damn the misborn.* He'd followed through on his threat to her and Lingiari. She stopped in her tracks. Lingiari. If Haggardy had punished her for refusing to cover up for him, had he punished the pilot too?

Did Lingiari already know he'd been blacklisted, and did he blame her for pushing him to tell the truth? Was that why he hadn't been answering her mails?

Jas continued on her way back to her apartment. When she arrived, she threw herself on her bed. Her plans to get away from Earth were falling through, and it looked like a good friend now hated her. Could the day get any worse?

As she lay thinking about what other spacework she could apply for and wondering how far Haggardy's reach stretched, her interface pinged again. Lifting her arm from across her eyes, she peered at the screen. She blinked away the blurriness of her vision. Someone was calling her on a live vidmail.

She sat up and squinted at the name. When she recognized it, she smiled. Finally, she had something to be happy about. She thumbed the icon to open the vid.

"Jas," exclaimed Makey as soon as he saw her.

"Hi, what's up, kid? How are you doing?"

The young man looked much better than he had when

Jas had last seen him. His face had filled out, and his skin was a healthy color.

"I'm all right. I'm living in a holding center while they process my refugee application. Some of the people here say I shouldn't have any problems because Dawn's being invaded at the moment. Did you hear they're sending in extra troops?"

"Yeah, I did. I hope they win back the planet soon, Makey."

"So do I." He paused and screwed up his face as if he found it difficult to say his following words. "I'm worried about my da. I know he wasn't good to me, but..."

"I understand. He's still your father. Try not to worry. I'm sure the army's doing everything they can to protect Dawn's inhabitants."

"And I miss Mam and Neeve. When they got taken by the Shadows...and I left so fast...what had happened to them didn't really sink in. Now I've had time to think about it..." The kid's expression fell.

"I'm sorry, Makey," Jas said. "But, you know, I think they would have been happy to know that you got away, and that you're going to have a chance at a new life."

Makey smiled sadly. "Yeah, maybe."

"So, what's the plan when your application's approved?" Jas asked.

"I haven't decided. There's so much I don't know, and so much I want to do. But I was...I was thinking about becoming a security officer like you. I want to fight the Shadows, Jas. I want to get them back for what they did to my family and my friends. It might help me feel better about leaving them on Dawn if I could work at protecting other people."

"Makey, you've got nothing to feel bad about—"

"I know. I know. I understand what you and Carl said about me being just a kid and everything. But it doesn't change how I feel. Jas, could you help me? I don't know anyone here, and I need someone to help me apply for courses, or maybe apply to the military. I haven't decided yet exactly what I want to do."

She arranged to go and see him at the refugee center. It would be good to see him again, and it would give her something to occupy her while she figured out what she was going to do with the rest of her life, too.

6

Carl sat in the kitchen of his parents' farmhouse. Though the weather was as hot as an oven outside, the room felt cold to him. It was twilight, but he hadn't turned on the lights. He preferred the dark. It matched his feelings, and artificial illumination only seemed to drive home the fact that his parents weren't there. From outside came a kookaburra's laughter and the songs of cicadas, driving away the unwelcome silence.

Carl's eyes were sandy and sore, and his head throbbed. He couldn't remember the last time he'd slept properly since finding out that his parents had gone missing. After the initial shock and visits to the police, as well as anyone else who might provide a clue as to what had happened, his sleep had been invaded by dreams of his mum and dad.

His sleeping mind jumbled up his parents with the events of his time aboard the *Galathea*. He would dream of fighting to get over to the Shadow of Grantwise, the former pilot, and take over the flight controls before the starship crashed. But when the Shadow turned around, it was his father. Or he would see Makey take aim at the Shadow that had been about to kill Harrington on Dawn, but the Shadow would transform into his mother. Whenever he woke, sweating, from the nightmares, he would always ask himself the same questions:

Had his parents been taken by Shadows? Was Earth being invaded?

He didn't have any evidence for his fears, and all that he knew about Shadows contradicted the idea. If Shadows had taken his parents, he would have expected to find replicants in their place. And if Shadows were on the farm, he would have expected to find their traps. But he'd checked every meter of the familiar soil and found nothing but weeds and the remains of unharvested crops.

The only explanation for his parents' disappearance the police could offer was that they'd gone for a walk—their car was in the garage—and they'd had an accident. It was also remotely possible that they'd been attacked or abducted, though crimes like that were unheard of in the area.

Carl couldn't accept the police's conclusions. His parents knew their surroundings too well to go anywhere unsafe or do anything dangerous. And they were fit and healthy for their ages. The idea that both of them could suddenly collapse, with neither of them able to get help, just wasn't credible.

Over the last few days, Carl hadn't paused in his search for them. He'd tramped the landscape, calling them both by name, and flown his dad's old plane over the whole farm. He'd spoken to everyone who could possibly have seen them before they disappeared. He'd read everything he could on what had been happening in the area at the time, hoping to find something—anything—that might be remotely related.

Nothing. He'd found nothing that might lead him to the

two people who meant the most in the world to him. It was as though they'd eaten breakfast, tidied up the kitchen, gone out, and stepped off a cliff into a sea that swept them away, leaving no trace.

As he sat in the dark, a deep fatigue came over Carl. He put his head on the table, resting it on his folded arms, and fell asleep.

In the middle of the night, a pinging awakened him. It was coming from the interface he'd fallen asleep on. Wincing from a crick in his neck, he sat up and checked the screen. It was an advertisement. *Great.* He was about to try to go back to sleep when he saw a message below the ad. It had arrived that morning from Harrington.

It had to have been the fourth or fifth time she'd mailed him. He'd put off replying because it felt like the moment he talked to someone who didn't know his parents were missing, and told them the news, it would make it all real. He'd hoped that when he finally answered her messages, it would be to tell her about the crisis in the past tense, with his mum and dad safe and sound beside him.

But he couldn't put off answering her any longer. He swiped the screen. As he read the message, his face fell. She was leaving already, going off on another mission. Between the lines, he read her frustration about the findings of the investigation into the *Galathea* incident. He'd barely registered the information when it had arrived, being too preoccupied with his parents' disappearance, but he could imagine how disappointing the result would be to the security officer.

He was sad that he hadn't had the chance to speak to her again before she left. He would miss her, and it would have been good to have someone to talk to about his fears for his parents. And though it hardly seemed important at that moment, he also hadn't completely given up on the idea that she might one day be something more than a friend.

But maybe it wasn't too late to speak to her. She'd only sent the mail the previous morning. She might not have left yet. He spoke a quick reply into his interface, asking if she could talk. After checking the message on the screen, he hit send.

Almost immediately, he got a vidmail request. As he read the sender, he understood that it hadn't been too late. He accepted the request, and Harrington's face appeared on the screen. He didn't think he'd ever felt happier to see her.

"Woah. Is something wrong?" was the first thing she said. "Sorry, Lingiari, but you look kratting terrible."

"It's a long story, Harrington. I'd tell you all about it, but I dunno if you have time. Are you shipping out soon?"

"Huh. No, I'm not. And you might not be either, sorry. But tell me what's happened there first. Are your folks okay?"

"No, they're...they're..." He fought to control himself.

"Krat, Lingiari. What's wrong?"

He passed a hand over his eyes. "If you aren't going anywhere soon, do you think you could come out here? Something's happened, and I can't make any sense of it."

"Of course. I'll be there on the next shuttle."

7

———

Jas had never been to Australia. As the shuttle descended to the spaceport, she realized that she'd seen more of other planets than she'd seen of Earth. Most of her childhood had been spent on Mars. It was only when she'd reached puberty that it had occurred to the orphanage director that if she didn't go to Earth soon, she would grow too tall and weak to ever go there. A few more years in a government institution in Chicago had passed, then she'd gone directly to security training and as soon as she'd graduated, she left on her first mission aboard a prospector.

At the time, she'd seen no reason not to start work immediately. She had no family nor any particularly close friends to leave behind, but as she looked out of the shuttle window at the bright blue of Botany Bay and the thin, white-yellow line of the beaches along the New South Wales coast, she wondered if she should have spent more time exploring the home planet of humankind. Maybe it wasn't such a bad thing that she'd been forced to stay a while. At least she could help Carl search for his missing parents. Their disappearance was very odd, and he was naturally out of his mind with worry.

Jas grabbed the cabin bag that held the few things she'd brought with her and went directly out to meet her friend. He was easy to spot among the happy faces of the people waiting to meet other passengers. He was smiling like them, but he had dark shadows under his eyes, and he'd lost so much weight he looked positively gaunt.

"Thanks for coming," he said as she approached. After a welcoming hug, he pulled something out from his jacket. "These are for you." It was a pair of flight goggles.

Jas took them from his hand. "Don't tell me we're going to—"

"The family plane's the fastest way to get home. Unless you're tired of flying after your trip?"

"No, I'd love to have a ride in your plane."

"Great. Let's go over to the airport," Carl said. "The place is a lot quieter than it used to be. More and more people take the shuttle these days."

Carl's plane looked out of place among the expensive, gleaming hobby aircraft at the airport. Jas was no expert on airplanes, but she would have bet money that it was from the previous century. A simple two-seater, its paint was dull, and the fuselage was patched in places. But she liked the look of it. There was something about it that explained a lot about Carl.

He helped her up into the passenger seat. As he got in, she stowed her bag in the footwell, fastened her safety harness, and put on her goggles. Carl checked over his shoulder that she was ready, and he started the engine.

What followed was one of the most memorable experiences of Jas's life. As they soared up into the cloudless sky, she understood why Carl loved flying so much. She'd never felt so free or exhilarated. The roar of the engine and the wind made it impossible to speak, but when her friend looked over his shoulder again, they shared a smile. Jas relaxed in her seat and gazed at the mountains at the edge of Sydney, content to be carried along in the plane.

A little while later but too soon, it seemed, they were descending. She could see fields, a narrow road edged with trees, a house, and a flat, open place that she supposed served as an airstrip. Her bones were rattled as they landed on the bare dirt.

Carl took her over to his family home: a two-story, wide, wooden house. Once they were inside the cool interior, he showed her to the guest bedroom and left her to freshen up after her journey. She went to the bathroom and washed off the dirt that had accumulated on her face around the goggles before returning to the bedroom to unpack.

The room was simple, old-fashioned, and cozy. On the wall hung a photograph of a tall, part-Aboriginal man and a blonde, fair-skinned woman with their arms around a gawky, teenage Carl. Jas's heart ached at the thought of how her friend had to be feeling about his parents' disappearance. She also ached for the normal, loving childhood that she'd never known.

Downstairs, she found Carl in the large kitchen, his fingers sweeping an interface on the table. He looked up as she came in.

"Found any leads?" she asked.

He shook his head. "I've looked everywhere and so have their friends and the police. It's completely unlike them to just go off without telling someone, and they would never willingly let the farm fall into the state it's in. I can't help but think something terrible's happened."

Jas sat down opposite him and reached over to put her

hand on his. "I'm so sorry. I'll do everything I can to help. What was the place like when you got here? Did it look like there'd been a fight?"

"No. Everything looked normal. Like they'd just gone out for a walk and hadn't come back."

They talked on, discussing each possible reason for the disappearance and dismissing each in turn. Outside, the sky darkened as evening began to fall. Carl turned on the light and made them both dinner. As they ate, they continued to discuss the problem. What could persuade an older couple who had busy lives including daily duties to keep their farm going, to simply up and leave?

An answer, based on her and Carl's experiences aboard the *Galathea,* nagged at the back of Jas's mind. She didn't name it, though. She didn't want to make the suggestion to her friend.

They had both been silent for some time, Jas realized, when Carl asked if she would like to take a walk with him around the farm before it got too dark.

"I'd love to," she replied.

The air felt thick and warm as they stepped out into the twilight. Cicadas sang loudly. All color had left with the setting of the sun, and the farm looked mysterious and other-worldly in shades of gray and black. They went through the yard and up a short slope that led to the fields. Trees rose tall and slim at their edges, and they followed a track toward them.

"This leads to the upper paddock," Carl said, "where Mum taught me to ride."

"You can ride horses too? That's amazing. I can't even drive a car."

"Yeah, I can. Though I learned so long ago I can't really remember. But I've seen the pictures of Mum teaching me.

They don't keep horses any more. They sold them all when I left to go to flight school. I think they must have only been keeping them for my benefit."

"They sound like great parents."

"Yeah, they're good people. No one had anything but good to say about them when I went around the neighborhood making inquiries. Some people said how much they would be missed, like they didn't expect to see them again." Carl's voice dried up. Jas touched his upper arm.

They were under the trees, walking through the leaf litter and fallen bark. The rustle their steps made echoed the sound of the breeze in the long, thin branches and leaves above them.

Carl stopped, his head hung low, as if he hadn't the will to go farther. Jas waited beside him, her hand still gently touching his arm. After a moment, the pilot looked up, and his face was illuminated by the light of the rising moon. Jas could see glints in his dark eyes as he looked intently at her. He turned his body toward her and held her arms.

As he leaned closer, Jas closed her eyes, waiting for his kiss.

But a screech broke through the air, and she heard the flapping of wings. Carl exclaimed, and Jas opened her eyes. Flux had landed on his head.

"G'day, Jas," the creature said. "Carl, you didn't say we were having visitors."

8

———

"This is some place," Carl said as they drove up the long, wide driveway toward Sayen's home four days later. Magnolia trees in flower bordered the pavement, their huge, creamy goblet-shaped flowers cupped toward the sky. "Sayen told me her family was well off, but I didn't think she meant *this* well off."

Jas had spoken into an intercom at the gates before their autocab had been allowed through. From there, it had been a five-minute drive through immaculate grounds to the house, or rather, the mansion. The cab stopped and they got out.

Jas didn't normally ever think about the clothes she wore or how she looked, but it was impossible not to feel a little self-conscious in such an intimidating setting.

One of a pair of huge doors opened, and a maid in a traditional black and white uniform appeared. "Good afternoon, madam, sir. Would you please step this way?"

They followed the maid as she led them across a wood-paneled, wood-floored—*real* wood—hallway and through several sumptuous sitting rooms. Jas had a feeling that each room had a special name. That was the lounge, that was the parlor, she decided as they passed them. That room was for the gentlemen to withdraw and smoke after dinner, and that one was for the ladies' morning sewing circle. It was like a film set.

The maid took them into a conservatory at the back of the house. It filled with orchids of all shapes, sizes, and colors. Somewhere out of sight, a fountain played.

Sayen was lying in a chaise longue next to the glass outer wall, an animal on her lap, accompanied by a woman in a wicker chair. Jas guessed the woman had to be Sayen's mother, though she didn't look much older than her daughter. Enough money could buy very effective anti-aging therapies. At the sight of them, the woman got up.

"Ms. Harrington, we met at the hospital, I believe, while Sayen was recuperating? How wonderful to see you again," she said. "And you must be Mr. Lingiari. Please, come and sit down, both of you. What can Jessica get you to drink?"

Sayen looked stronger than she had when Jas had last seen her. She sat up and smiled. "Hi. It's great to see you. Thanks for coming."

After a few minutes' small talk, Sayen gently hinted to her mother that she should leave her alone with her friends, and the woman left, telling them to ask Jessica for anything they wanted. Anything at all.

As soon as the woman was out of earshot, Sayen said, "The maid's name is Florence, and she appreciates it if you call her that. Mama calls all our maids Jessica. She says it's because she can't remember their names. It's so embarrassing."

"You look amazing," said Carl. "It's hard to believe you were in such a bad way."

"Thanks, Carl. I feel pretty good. I'm nearly back to normal. I had to learn to do just about everything again. But I'm not complaining. I'm grateful to be here. And that reminds me..." She turned to Jas. "I never thanked you properly for what you did for me. Not long after I woke up in stasis, Carl told me that it was you who saved me. He said it was you who refused to give up when everyone else was saying I was a goner. If it weren't for you, I wouldn't be here. I'll never forget that, and, believe me, neither will my parents."

Jas struggled to think of what to say. "It wasn't anything—"

"Shut up, Harrington," said Carl. "You were a bloody hero."

Then she *really* didn't know what to say. The best option seemed to be to change the subject. "Thanks. I mean it. But we haven't only come here to see you, Sayen. We wanted to talk to you about something face to face."

Sayen sat up straighter. "Really? What is it? This sounds interesting. I've been so bored while I've been recuperating. Tell me what it is."

The eager anticipation on her face changed to sorrow and concern as Lingiari told her about his missing parents. He spoke for several minutes, and after he finished, no one spoke for a while.

"Carl, I'm so sorry," Sayen said quietly.

"I went over to his parents' place to help him," Jas said. "It's exactly like he says. It's totally weird. They've vanished into thin air, and no one's noticed anything suspicious. Not at the time they went missing nor since.

"You're the smartest person we know, Sayen. We were wondering if you could think of anything we or the police haven't done yet to find out what's happened to them. No creds have been taken out of their bank accounts since the last time they were seen. They lived in the same place all their lives, and everyone in the area knew them, but no one has any idea what could have happened."

"It *is* very strange," Sayen said. "Carl, I don't want to scare you, but do you think that it might have something to do with the Shadows?"

"I do," he replied. "We both do," he added, glancing at Jas. "Though it doesn't make a lot of sense. My parents haven't been replaced. They're just gone. And what would the Shadows want with them? They're just farmers."

Sayen's expression was troubled. "It might not be your parents they want. It could be their land. The Shadows need places for their traps, places not too far from human habitations, but not so close that they'd be easily discovered."

"Yeah, I had the same thought, to be honest. I flew all over the farm, but there's nothing there."

The word *yet* hung in the air, unspoken.

"When we arrived back on Earth," said Jas, "we were given the same tests that we went through on Dawn. *Dawn*, which was invaded by Shadows. I told them there might be a Shadow on the ship, but they said the tests were foolproof. How could they be foolproof if a Shadow got onto Dawn?"

"Yeah. And if they got onto Dawn, maybe they're here," said Lingiari.

"I've been thinking about what happened on K. 67092d and Dawn," Sayen said. "There's so much that doesn't add up. How long has the government known about Shadows? Long enough for them to set up at least two testing centers, on Dawn and here, for people exposed to them, but I haven't seen anything in the media about them. Have you? I've been searching for days. Why are they keeping the Shadows a secret? Do all the prospecting companies know about them? Is the government doing anything to stop them from spreading? Are the Transgalactic Council and Unity involved?"

"They made us sign a secrecy agreement on Dawn," Jas said. "It was really shady. And they wouldn't tell us what they did with any Shadows they caught."

Sayen frowned. "There has to be a way we can find out."

She rose from her seat and the animal on her lap jumped down. Lingiari gazed after it as it trotted away. "Is that a dog or a cat?"

"Neither, or both," said Sayen, "depending on how you look at it. Beau's a cag, or a dot. I don't know what the official word is."

"It's a hybrid cat and dog?"

"Yes, he is. He was a present to welcome me home. He's soft as a cat to cuddle, but loyal as a dog. He doesn't scratch up the furniture, and he takes himself for walks if you want. And you can teach him tricks. He's the ideal pet."

She opened the French doors, and Beau ran outside. They stepped into the garden—except her family garden was more like a park. A lush, vivid green grass carpet flowed down a slight incline at the back of the house and out as far as the eye could see. Ornamental trees dotted the verdant expanse, and in the distance was a bright, silvery lake with...Jas stopped. It couldn't be.

"Are those flamingoes?" she asked, pointing at the moving pink dots on the watery expanse.

"Yeah," Lee replied in a mildly abashed tone, as if she'd been asked the question many times before and found the admission a little shameful. "Do y'all want to come with me for my daily walk?"

"Hey, the temperature's cooled down a lot," Lingiari said.

"It's..." He looked up at the cloudless sky, leaving his sentence hanging.

Lee sighed. "It's air-conditioned."

"It's what?" said Jas. "You mean...the whole place?"

"Yeah. I sometimes forget how it must seem to strangers."

"But, how?" asked Lingiari.

"There's a force field dome over the house and grounds. You drove through it, but you wouldn't have noticed. Underground machines cool the air, and the dome prevents the air inside from mixing with the air outside."

"Woah," Lingiari said. "Can you fly through it?"

"Yeah. I could explain how the force field works, but it's a little complicated."

"That's okay," Jas said. If Sayen found the explanation complicated, it would be beyond her and Lingiari's understanding. "Where do you want to walk?"

"I usually go to the lake and back. My mama and daddy get antsy if I go too far. I have to stay in sight of the house."

"I guess what happened to you was pretty tough on them," said Jas.

"You don't know the half of it. My mama always wanted to wrap me in cotton wool, but my daddy encouraged me to spread my wings. Now, they're both the same. It's like I'm five years old again."

Lingiari had drawn a little ahead of them. Jas wondered if he was going to trip over his feet because he wasn't looking where he was going. He was looking upward, as if trying to spot the force field holding the cool air in. The pilot stopped and turned. "Hey, I just remembered something. When you were breaking the comm links on the *Galathea's* defense units, you said you used to tamper with the android servants at home. Is Florence an android?"

"Yeah, she is. They all are. Me, mama, and daddy are the only humans in the house."

"You're kidding," exclaimed Jas. It was her turn to stop in her tracks. "Then, what was all that about her preferring to be called by her name? You're saying they have feelings?"

"Our androids aren't like your defense units, Jas. The ratio of human cells to synthetic components is much higher than usual. They aren't commercially available. To be honest, they sit the border of the legislation on android ethics. But they've always seemed happy to me. And it's better than using humans for menial work, don't you think?"

Lingiari asked the question that was also on Jas's lips. "Sayen, what the hell do your parents do? I mean, if it's okay to ask."

"You know, that's a good question, Carl. I wish I knew. When I was younger, I tried asking them a few times. My brother and I had a competition going to see who'd be the first to figure it out. But they always said it was better that I didn't know." She smiled a little wistfully. "It's something that brings in a lot of money, that's for sure. My grandparents aren't nearly so well off.

"And my parents know plenty of important people. We've had all kinds of visitors over the years—people on the news, celebrities, government ministers, heads of global corporations, and so on."

They were nearing the lake. The flamingoes looked almost unreal. Their feathers were the color of fairy floss, and they were standing on one stick-like leg each. Jas thought she'd heard that they were extinct in the wild.

She'd often heard the phrase, *how the other half live*, but Sayen's family didn't belong to the other half, they belonged a tiny fraction of the very richest of Earth's population. It was lucky for the navigator, and maybe, with her family connections, it would be lucky for them too in their quest to find out about the Shadows.

9

———

Sayen studied her reflection in her dressing room mirror. She wanted to look smart and professional. Her silver-blue pant-suit achieved just the right effect, she concluded. The color looked good against her blonde hair, and the suit's lines were neat and fitted her figure perfectly. If she wanted her interviewer to take her seriously, she would have to look the part, even if she had no intention of staying in the job longer than it took her to snoop behind the scenes, and even if her mama and daddy had told her she didn't even need to interview.

They'd pleaded with her not to go back to work, but when they'd finally relented, they'd said any job that she wanted was hers, providing she had the skills and qualifications. She only had to ask and they would arrange it. But she couldn't risk the Global Government thinking she was there for any other reason than that she wanted to work. She didn't want to be observed beyond the normal level of interest in a new employee.

She made a final check of her appearance before going downstairs to say goodbye to her parents. They were each in their home offices. Her mother was reading something. As she looked up, it was clear she'd been crying.

"Sayen," her mother said as she went in, "for the last time, why? Why can't you stay here and have fun doing whatever you want? You know that you only have to give the word, and we'll make it happen for you."

"Mama, I told you. What I want is a job. I'm dying stuck in here all day. Can't you at least try to understand that?"

"I'm trying, honey, I'm trying. But when I think of seeing you after your accident..."

"But I got better, didn't I? I'm better than ever. And I want to *do* something with my life. Not spend it hiding away from the tiniest little thing that might hurt me."

"Oh, sweetheart, I'm just worried about you. And when you have kids of your own you'll know how I feel."

"I'm sorry, Mama. Can you at least wish me well?"

"Of course I wish you well. I always wish you well, honey. Come and give your mama a hug."

Sayen's father didn't say anything to her when she went to see him. She was interrupting a vidcall. He asked the person he was speaking with to excuse him for a moment, and he came over to Sayen and wrapped his arms around her. After planting a kiss on her head, he turned back to the screen, giving her a half wave. He hadn't gone on and on trying to dissuade her like her mama had, but she could tell he was just as against the idea.

As she went downstairs and out to the chauffeur-driven heli that awaited her, she tried to ease her guilt at making her parents worry about her with the thought that, though it was true she really did want to get out of the house and start working again, she also had a more serious and less selfish reason for applying for the government job.

THE DOWNDRAFT from the heli messed up her hair as she got out on the roof of the GGSHQ, or Global Government Security Headquarters. It was a stroke of luck that the place was within an hour by heli from Sayen's family property. She didn't think her parents were ready yet to agree to her living away from home, if they would ever be.

A man in a suit was holding open a door, and she crossed the roof to go through it as the heli took off. The man smiled at her, and they went down in the elevator. Sayen thought he looked familiar. The more she glimpsed him from the corners of her eyes, the surer she was that she knew him, but she couldn't remember from where. She was sure that if she saw him in the right context, she would know him right away, but there, he seemed out of place. Or was her confusion an effect of the mind transfer treatment she'd undergone?

She faced the man. "Excuse me, do I know you?"

"I don't think so, ma'am," he replied.

They'd reached their floor, and the doors opened. The man told her the room number as Sayen stepped out, but he didn't accompany her. He remained in the elevator as the doors closed, and Sayen was left none the wiser. She shrugged. Maybe she would get a chance to talk to him later if she got the job. What was she thinking? Of course she'd get the job. She only had to go through the motions.

THE MINISTER for Global Security was a large woman. In her expansive kaftan and long, straightened hair, she didn't really look like she was responsible for the security of every living human being on the planet, but her manner made up for her relaxed dress code. When Sayen was shown into her office, the woman didn't look up from her interface for several long moments.

Sayen wondered if she should cough or something. She hadn't expected this kind of reception.

"Sit down," said the woman without looking up.

Sayen sat opposite her and folded her hands in her lap, wondering if she was in for a long wait.

The woman swiped her interface, and the screen turned black. Only then did she lift her head. She looked into Sayen's eyes for an uncomfortably long time.

"Sayen Lee," she said.

"Yes, ma'am, I'm here for—"

"I know why you're here." She reactivated her interface and brought up a new screen. After scanning the information, she glanced at Sayen and then back at the screen.

"You served aboard the *Galathea,* a prospecting starship belonging to Polestar Corp, which visited the planets K. 67092d and Dawn, among others. You were critically injured." She looked at Sayen again. "It says here that you made a full recovery." Her gaze roved Sayen's face and the upper half of her body. Sayen shrank a little at this frank inspection, but she supposed the woman had to be sure she was fit to work.

"Yes, ma'am. I'm completely well again."

"Your personal record stands up to scrutiny, and your qualifications and transcripts are excellent. There doesn't seem any doubt in your ability to perform your duties after the relevant training. Very well. I accept your application. Your employment begins Monday. Your position is probationary for six months."

The interview seemed to be over. The Minister for

Global Security hadn't asked her if she had any questions. Didn't they *always* ask if you had any questions? Sayen rose from her seat uncertainly.

As she went toward the door, the woman spoke. "Talk to my secretary. He'll tell you where your office is and anything else you need to know."

"Uh, thanks. Goodbye."

The woman didn't reply.

Sayen closed the door and went down the hallway. That had to be the quickest interview she'd ever had. She poked her head in at the first open door. An older man in an expensive navy blue suit sat at a desk inside the room. His hair and beard were snowy white and closely clipped.

"Hello," he said in a British accent. "You must be Ms. Lee." He stood and went to Sayen to shake her hand.

After her frosty experience in the Minister for Global Security's office, she was relieved by the man's kindly smile that crinkled the skin around his eyes. Though she only intended to stay in the job as long as she needed to, she hadn't relished the thought of spending even a short time working there if they were all like the kaftan-wearing woman. Then she scolded herself for the thought. Hadn't she decided she wanted to take risks and do more challenging things with her life?

"Yes, that's me," she said.

"Wonderful. I'm Mr. Lombard, but you can call me Bernie. Do come and sit down, and we'll go over everything so you're ready to hit the ground running on Monday."

Sayen took a seat next to the man, and he explained the ins and outs of her role. Cyber intelligence seemed as interesting and difficult as she'd imagined it would be.

After they'd been speaking for a while, Sayen felt

comfortable enough to ask Bernie about their boss. "Is the Minister always so...formal?"

"Hmm...I understand why you ask. You see, things are quite tense around here at the moment. We're dealing with threats on several fronts, which you'll find out about as you begin your job. In fact, I and a few others would usually be the ones conducting the interviews for positions like yours, but the Minister has taken it upon herself to speak to each applicant individually, and double-check all the background searches we do on them. It's admirable, really. We can't take the slightest risk when it comes to global security."

"Oh, I understand."

"I'm sure you do. Shall we carry on? We have quite a bit to get through this morning."

"Yes, of course."

As she listened to Bernie telling her what information she was to look for and how she was to look for it, Sayen made a mental note every time she heard anything that might lead her to the Shadows.

10

___

Carl had returned to Australia, but he was regretting his decision. There seemed to be nothing he could do there, and waiting for Sayen to investigate the possibility of there being Shadows on Earth was agonizing. Every moment that passed increased his chances of never seeing his parents again. Every moment might mean the difference between life and death. He wondered if he would be more useful on the other side of the world with Sayen and Harrington.

Unable to bear the quiet, empty farmhouse any longer, he'd rented a small flat in Sydney, close to the spaceport in case he needed to be somewhere in a hurry. Flux had stayed on at the farm in case anything new turned up. The little fella could get into places and see things that would be impossible for a human. If he had anything to report, he would tell Mrs. Jesson, who would then contact Carl.

At first, the messages that had arrived from Sayen had been discouraging. She hadn't been able to find out anything about the Shadows, even though in her role she had access to highly classified material. Along with Jas, they'd concluded that it was very strange, considering that they were a known threat. The Global Government had commissioned Dawn as a quarantine and testing area, and scientists on Earth were testing exposed arrivals from deep space. So Shadows weren't that much of a secret. But no one was talking about them, and the government hadn't seemed to hold any information on them.

Then Sayen had discovered that there were hidden files —files that even she wasn't supposed to know about. They'd agreed they had to contain something worth knowing. But for days on end, Sayen hadn't been able to get into them. Each day that she failed, Carl had been more and more convinced that the files had to contain what they were looking for. If someone of Sayen's caliber couldn't crack them, they had to be something very special.

Carl was out walking the waterfront at The Rocks when the call came. He took out his interface. Jas was requesting a vidcall. Could this be it? Had Sayen uncovered the truth about the Shadows? He pressed the accept key, and Jas appeared on the screen.

"Sayen's gone missing," she exclaimed.

"What? She...how?" he asked.

"Carl, can you get over here? Her parents are going crazy. They want us to go and see them. They won't talk over any messaging service. They're insisting on speaking to us face to face."

"I'll be there as soon as I can. Meet me at the spaceport, and we'll go from there. I'm hanging up now to call a cab. Be careful, Jas. If anything's happened to Sayen because she was snooping, you and I could both be in danger."

～

Mrs. Lee looked very different from the last time Carl had seen her. When they arrived at the door, she let them in herself. Her face had lost its color except for her eyes, which were red-rimmed. She was a ghost of her former self, as if all life had been drained from her. Mr. Lee was waiting in the first room they came to. He was trying to put on a brave front, but it was clear that beneath the veneer, he was crumbling.

"Thank you for coming so quickly," said Mr. Lee. "Please, sit down."

"It's no problem," said Carl. "Has there been any word from Sayen?"

"Nothing," Mrs. Lee said. "Not a single sight or sound of her since yesterday evening."

Harrington said, "Is it possible she—"

"Ms. Harrington," said Mrs. Lee. "Let me show you something." She handed over an interface. On the screen was a message from Sayen to her mother, saying that she would be spending the weekend with a friend, and her mother was not to worry about her. "It's a lie."

"Something's happened to her," Mr. Lee said. "You two seem close with Sayen, and I've a feeling you might know something about it." He held up a hand to silence Harrington as she began to speak. "We don't have time for denials. We have to get our daughter back, and we need you to help us."

"I wasn't about to deny anything, Mr. Lee," Harrington said. "We'll do all we can to help."

"I'm certainly glad to hear it. Please begin by telling me what *you* think might be the reason for her disappearance."

Carl and Harrington explained about the Shadows.

"Yes." Mrs. Lee nodded. "Sayen did tell us what had

happened on her last mission. And you really think they might have something to do with what's happened to my daughter?"

Carl went on to tell the couple about his missing parents and his and Harrington's suspicions that there might be some kind of cover-up going on about Shadows on Earth. He told them that Sayen had been trying to uncover information in the Global Government's databanks. By the time he'd finished, Sayen's parents' expressions were grave. Mrs. Lee put her face in her hands.

"I'd heard the rumors, Carleen," said Mr. Lee. "We both had. If only we'd known what she was trying to do. We could have stopped her. Why oh why did I help her get that job?"

"You mean you already knew about the Shadows?" Carl asked.

"No, we didn't," said Mrs. Lee, raising her head, "but we knew something was going on that we weren't being told about. Craven and I work for the Government. We've been in the job for over thirty years, and we know it inside out. A few months ago, we began to suspect that we were being deprived of information and excluded from certain meetings. Any subtle inquiries we made were met with silence and a closing of the ranks. There was obviously something big and highly sensitive going on. It must have been to do with these Shadows." She looked upward as if in supplication. "Dear Lord, if I'd known Sayen was getting herself mixed up in governmental intrigues, I would never have let her get involved."

"These people..." Mr. Lee looked gravely at Carl and Harrington. "You have no idea what they're capable of."

"My little girl," said Mrs. Lee softly. "Craven, what are we going to do?"

"Everything we can, Carleen. We're going to do everything we can to get her back. We still have friends. Don't forget that.

"Mr. Lingiari, Ms. Harrington, we need your help. Sayen has touched on something sensitive, and she's been taken. Whoever it was who took her, they have to be very high up. It has to be people who are confident that their actions will be beyond reproach. There aren't many who are above our circles of influence. Thank you for being frank with us. Now that we know what Sayen was doing, we can begin to turn the wheels that will bring these people's actions to light.

"Unfortunately, for the time being, we can't leave our home. Due to our connection to Sayen, the chances are that these individuals may try to take us too. We can't do a thing in person to go get to our baby girl. We would ask her brother to bring her back, but he's at the other end of the galaxy."

"Wait a minute, are you saying you know where she is?" Carl asked.

"We do," Mrs. Lee replied. "We know exactly where she is. She's on an air transport, and it's out over the Atlantic, heading toward Africa. We're keeping track of it." In response to Carl and Harrington's surprised expressions, she went on, "When Sayen was undergoing her cloning treatment, we had a tracer inserted into her body. Was it overstepping the mark? Yes. Was it invading her privacy? You betcha. Do I regret it? Not for a second." She gazed at them defiantly.

"Whatever the rights and wrongs of what we did," said Mr. Lee, "if we hadn't done it, I doubt we'd ever see our darlin' again."

"Where is she?" Carl asked. "We'll get her back."

"Come with me," Mrs. Lee said, rising. "I'll show you

how to trace her and give you anything else you need. Whatever it might be, just ask."

11

—————

Sayen sat in darkness. She was hot. Stripping down to her underwear had provided some relief, but not much. Though her enhanced skin provided some protection from the heat inside the box where the Shadows had put her, breathing in the hot air had raised her body temperature to uncomfortable levels.

She guessed the box wasn't much more than a meter in every direction. The ceiling was too low for her to stand up, and the walls were too close together for her to lie down outstretched. They were made of metal, and they were warm to the touch. There was no ventilation.

That morning, when she'd arrived for work, the Minister had been out of the office. Sayen had been glad because it meant she would be left to her regular work without being interrupted to research something in particular. She'd anticipated the opportunity to exploit the crack she'd found in the security surrounding the files on the Shadows. She'd thought she'd disabled any unauthorized access alerts. She'd been wrong.

After only minutes of reading, wide-eyed, the files on the

Shadows, Bernie had entered her office without knocking. Gone were his twinkling eyes and cheery expression. It had all been a facade. Bernie had the expression of a corpse. As he'd grabbed her, two more men had come in, including the man who'd met her that first day whose face she couldn't place.

Sayen had fought, of course. She'd resisted with every ounce of her newly enhanced strength, but after she'd broken one of the men's arms, Bernie had knocked her out.

Blindfolded and with her wrists bound with wire, she'd come around aboard a heli, and they'd flown for seven or eight hours before touching down. She recalled stumbling through vegetation, the muzzle of a weapon of some kind pressed to her skull, before being pushed into the box.

Since then, she'd managed to work the blindfold off of her head, but as there was no light in the box, it made no difference to her. She still had little idea where she was, except that it was somewhere hot. From the length of the flight, she guessed she was somewhere in Africa.

The Shadows had her. She wondered how long she had before they would try to make a Shadow of her too. That would not happen. She wouldn't let it. The thought of a Shadow Sayen returning home to her parents turned her stomach. She would rather die than expose them to danger.

She was dizzy with the heat, and her skin was slick with sweat. She licked her arm to try to relieve her dry, swollen mouth. She stopped mid-lick. What had she been thinking? She was forgetting her physical enhancements. Maybe she could break out of her prison.

Sayen wasted no time. She'd located the door by feeling the walls, and she'd pushed it once before. This time she *really* pushed it. The metal bent under the pressure she applied, but the door didn't open. Sayen shifted back in the box. Bracing herself against the opposite wall, she put both her feet against the door and pushed with her legs. As she gasped with the effort, the door buckled. Bright light streamed through chinks on either side. She'd nearly gotten it open.

Bending her knees, Sayen drew up her legs. She spread her arms for balance and gave the door a massive kick. Whatever was holding it closed broke, and the door flew open, revealing lush vegetation. The rich, 'green' aroma of the jungle rushed in.

The daylight was incredibly bright after the hours she'd spent in pitch darkness, but Sayen's enhanced eyes reacted to the change immediately.

Outside, someone shouted.

Sayen scrambled out of the box. She was in a clearing of knee-high grass and plants, bordered in the distance by tall trees hung with moss and vines. Figures were running toward her across the clearing. The nearest escape route seemed to be the forest. She set off toward the trees at a sprint, heading for the safety of the darkness between the trunks.

She heard more shouts coming from behind her. Time seemed to slow down. Every step she took, she expected to feel the pain of a laser burn. Would she feel the beams hitting her, or would it all be over before she knew what had happened? She was running fast, faster than an unenhanced human could ever run. Another ten seconds and she would make it. She could hardly believe her luck had lasted so long. Why weren't the Shadows shooting?

Then it came. Something exploded against her back, and suddenly she couldn't feel her legs. The impetus of her running carried her forward, and she found herself sliding through the vegetation face down. A horrible slicing sensation across her face and the bare skin of her arms and legs were the last things she felt before she lost consciousness.

SOMETHING WAS TUGGING at her ankles, and her back hurt. Her back hurt a lot. Sayen opened her eyes to see a jungle canopy passing overhead, the blue sky visible in patches between the leaves and branches. She lifted her head to look forward. Two men were dragging her, holding one of her ankles each. She was being pulled down a track.

Her undershirt was pulled up, and the rough track was scraping the skin off her back. She felt like she was being shredded. She struggled violently and ripped her ankles out of the Shadows' grips. In a moment, she was up and running again.

But she didn't get far. That time, they were ready. Within moments, she felt another explosion against her back.

The next time she came around, she was lying on her front. The second thing she registered was pain from all over her body. She fought the urge to move. As soon as they knew she was awake, the Shadows would stun her again. She needed a better plan than running to get away.

Slowly, she opened her eyes. Blades of grass obscured her view. The blades were stained red, with her blood, she guessed. She wasn't inside a Shadow trap yet, at least.

Someone was approaching her. More than one person. Large, powerful hands grabbed her around the waist. She was lifted onto a man's shoulder. Sayen tried to remain limp so that the Shadow man would think she was still uncon-scious. She held her eyes only slightly open as she tried to take in as much of her surroundings as she could.

There was the structure she'd been expecting to see: the

hexagonal blocks of a Shadow trap, deep within an African jungle, where it would be easy to hide. The trees were close together, no doubt helping to screen the trap from the overhead view of planes and helis.

If she could just get a few seconds' head start on the Shadows, if she could just make it far enough that they wouldn't have a clear shot at her with a stunning laser beam, she could get away. From the sounds around her, Sayen guessed the man was accompanied by three or four more Shadows.

They'd reached the trap. As soon as they entered the hexagonal doorway, the cool interior raised goosebumps on Sayen's skin. She would have to act now, before it was too late.

The Shadow carrying her stopped, and his shoulders shifted as he moved to lower Sayen down. As his hands fastened around her and raised her, the man's head came into view. Sayen drove her elbow into the side of it. His skull swung away sharply, and there was a loud report as his neck cracked. His body jerking, the Shadow hit the floor. Sayen fell with him, but she broke away and landed on her feet.

The other Shadows were immediately upon her. She grabbed the nearest one and drove its head into the stony wall. Its cranium shattered, and the Shadow woman slid to the ground, leaving a trail of blood, hair, and brains.

Another Shadow had hold of Sayen. His arms wrapped over hers in a bear hug. Sayen broke his grip and was about to turn and attack him, but another Shadow kicked her feet out from under her. She fell. Her chin jarred against the floor, sending a shockwave through her head. Her mouth filled with blood.

As she tried to rise, she felt a third explosion in her back. *No*, she screamed inside. They'd stunned her again. She'd failed. She was going to die. She was facing the doorway. Bright green vegetation framed by a dark, hexagonal hole faded from her sight.

She was alive, but she could see nothing but darkness. Sayen reached out and felt familiar, smooth metal. She was in a box like the one the Shadows had put her in before. But she'd bent and broken that one. They must have put her in a new box.

Wincing, she sat up. Every inch of her was sore. Her lips felt funny. She put a hand to her mouth and found that it was swollen. Dried blood encrusted her chin.

Something must have gone wrong. The last thing she remembered was being inside a Shadow trap. They'd stunned her for the third time. She'd thought that the Shadows would kill her, and a new Sayen would appear. That was what people thought happened. Or had they got it wrong? Were the Shadows' victims kept in prison while their replacements took over their lives?

Feeling around the inside of the box, Sayen found the edge that marked the door. She kicked it with all her might, but the thing didn't move. She gasped in pain at the shock that ran up her legs. The Shadows must have reinforced the door somehow.

She kicked it again, but the door didn't move a centimeter. Exhausted and in pain, she flopped to the floor. So much for her enhancements. She was trapped.

A scraping sound came from outside. Sayen was thrown to one side as the box tilted. It was being lifted up. She swayed as the box was moved. She was being taken somewhere.

12

Carl looked out of the shuttle window as they sped back to London. Harrington was distracted, mailing someone on her interface. The last time they'd looked at the tracer dot that marked Sayen's location, it had shown she was in Gabon.

Far beneath, a dark seascape sped by. They were gaining on the sunrise, flying toward it over the ocean. He and Harrington had argued. He'd wanted to fly directly to Africa.

They didn't know how long they had before the Shadows killed and replicated Sayen, but Harrington had insisted that they needed to equip themselves properly before attempting a rescue. They would have only one chance, and they had to make it count.

Carl couldn't erase from his imagination the image of Sayen being taken into one of the Shadow traps. He hoped that the aliens would think twice before killing and replacing the daughter of one of Earth's most influential families. Whatever the creatures were, they weren't stupid.

In Carl's experience, they worked smartly, targeting the

top individuals in a hierarchy and keeping their actions secret as long as possible. There was a small chance that replacing Sayen with a Shadow was a risk they didn't want to take at that stage.

He suspected that the Shadows' method was to replace as much of a population as they could before they were discovered, and then subdue and replace the rest. Why they did it and what their ultimate plan was, he couldn't guess.

He wondered what Sayen had found out before she was taken.

Beside him in the shuttle's passenger cabin, Harrington closed her interface's screen and sat back.

"Did you get what you wanted?" Carl asked.

"Not yet. Someone's working on it. If he can get the stuff, it'll be ready by the time we arrive."

"So what is this stuff that's so important?"

Harrington gave him a sidelong glance. "Just stuff." When Carl raised his eyebrows, she added, "It might make all the difference. You know I wouldn't delay rescuing Sayen otherwise."

Carl sighed and returned to staring out the window. "Yeah, I know."

He wished the shuttle would go faster. He wished he was flying it. He would have them in London and then on to rendezvous with the heli that was carrying Sayen in no time. As well as his concern for his friend, his impatience was driven by the urge to find out more about the Shadows. He was desperate to locate his parents.

As soon as they were out of the spaceport in London, Carl and Harrington ran to catch an autocab to take them to meet her contact.

Harrington had arranged to meet him at an underpass not far from a freeway. The place was rank with the odor of stale piss and the acrid smell of unwashed bodies and clothes. The contact was accompanied by his mates, and they reminded Carl of the dero who had touched him for some creds the first night he'd arrived back on Earth. The groups of under-educated, under-privileged naturals seemed to be growing day by day. Carl wondered how they survived.

As the autocab pulled up, all but one stepped back, leaving a small man with dirty, balding hair and several days' beard growth standing alone. He had an old bag slung over his shoulder.

The autocab stopped, and Carl and Harrington got out. The small crowd of naturals drew back farther as Harrington stood to her full height. Carl had got used to her size, and though he was tall himself, he'd forgotten how imposing she was. In their current situation, among the kind of people present, it certainly came in handy.

The man with the bag looked up at Harrington. "I got it all. Everything you said."

"Let me see," said the security officer.

"All right." He took the bag off his shoulder and opened it. He held it at waist level, so that Harrington had to stoop to see inside. As she did so, the deros who had stepped back moved forward. *Drongos.* They didn't have the imagination to understand what the security officer would do to them if they attacked.

Carl also stepped forward, unzipping his jacket as he moved. He reached inside it and pulled out a weapon. Just the handle of it, enough to show the deros what he carried. At the sight of the weapon, they lowered their heads and shuffled back to their former position.

Harrington was inspecting the contents of the bag. She straightened up. "Got a reader?" she asked the man.

He pulled one from a capacious pocket. Harrington took the bag from the man and zipped it up. She held her wrist to the man's reader and typed in a figure. Nothing else was said.

Carl and Harrington got back into the cab and left. When the vehicle had left the underpass and was out on the freeway, Harrington turned to Carl.

"Can I see it?"

"What?"

"You know," she said, gesturing toward him.

"Harrington," Carl exclaimed, pretending to be shocked, "this isn't the time."

The security officer rolled her eyes, reached over and unzipped his jacket. She pulled out the weapon from its holster under his arm. "Thanks for helping me out back there. I thought you had to be showing them something when they all backed off."

"I think I was helping *them* out more than you."

"True." She nodded. "So, how in hell did you manage to bring this with you on two trips across the Atlantic, and I'm guessing, your flight from Australia too?"

"I have my ways."

Harrington smiled wryly. She studied the weapon. "Not bad," she said, handing it back. She patted the bag on her lap comfortingly. "But these are better. Hey, could you use your magical method to get these through security checks? I was going to use my professional license exemption, but your way sounds better. I don't want to risk a nosey Customs officer having a quick look."

"Sure, if you want."

A moment later, Harrington's interface beeped. A message had arrived for her. "Krat, " she said when she saw who it was from.

"What's wrong?"

"I've been mentoring Makey. He got his refugee status and he's started studying to be a security officer. I forgot I had to meet him this afternoon." She pressed accept, and the kid's familiar face appeared on the screen. Harrington explained that she was going away for a while and she would help him out when she got back.

The kid frowned. "Where are you going? Is that Carl with you? Hi, Carl."

"Hi, Makey," Carl replied. "Look, we're just going off on a short trip. Shouldn't be too long."

The kid didn't answer for a moment. "Are you going to...to...can I talk about secret stuff over a vidcall? Is it safe?"

"No, it isn't," Harrington said. "Makey, what's wrong?"

"Those things...we both know about. I think they're here."

"At the refugee center?" Carl asked.

The kid glanced to one side before nodding. "Are you going to fight them? Because if you are, I want to come with you."

"Makey, if those things are there," Carl said, "it isn't safe for you to stay. But we can't help you right now. We're in a hurry. Can you get away? We can find you when we get back."

"I think I can. I don't think they realize that I know what they are yet, but, wherever you're going, I want to come with you. I want to fight them too."

"Makey," said Harrington, "you're too young. It's much too dangerous for you to come with us."

"Please give me a chance," replied the kid. "I keep thinking of what happened to my mam and sister. I can't think straight anymore. I can't sleep. It's eating me up. Please let me help you."

As Carl struggled to find a way to ease Makey's conscience, the kid added, "You need me. There's only two of you. And I know what they're like. I saw the ones that replaced Neeve and Mam."

"You're right, Makey," Harrington said, with a nod of agreement from Carl. "We do need a third person. Okay, you're coming with us. Bring a change of clothes."

They arranged a corner to pick Makey up, then Harrington ended the vidcall. She brought up the screen that was tracing Sayen's tracker.

"They're moving her," she said. "She's left Africa, and she's traveling south."

Carl took the interface from Harrington to study the direction Sayen was going. The flashing dot was moving slowly but steadily away from the coast of South Africa. "Unless they're heading to an island, it looks like they're taking her to Antarctica."

Harrington had an inscrutable expression on her face.

13

―――

Hours later, they were in the air again, flying south to Antarctica. Harrington had been subdued the whole way from London. Carl wasn't sure if it was because she was worried about Sayen or if there was another reason. They couldn't talk about what they were about to do in case they were overheard by other passengers in the shuttle, but the woman also hadn't said a word about anything else.

Makey made up for Harrington's silence. He was excited to be taking part in their rescue attempt. As they were descending over McMurdo Sound, he said, "I read about this place in the refugee center. I've been catching up on information about Earth. They didn't teach us much about it on Dawn. All we learned was that humans had destroyed the environment and polluted the air. They taught us that humans had disrespected Earth Mother, and that she punished them by not allowing plants to grow and by bringing earthquakes and hurricanes."

"Well, that isn't completely wrong, apart from the Earth Mother part," Carl said. "The climate's still being affected by three hundred years of industrialization. The geography's changed a lot as the average temperature has risen. Antarctica's been melting for decades, and it hasn't stopped. Not likely to any time soon, either. You can't reverse rising global temperatures easily.

"It snowed here in the past, and at one time the whole continent was covered in massive sheets of ice. Now, the ice is only a hundred or so meters thick, and it's decreasing every summer. No more snow's fallen in years and it isn't likely to. It never did snow a lot in the first place. Looks like we've seen the last of it in our lifetimes."

Makey frowned as he looked out of the shuttle window over the semi-frozen continent.

McMurdo Sound was like a big country town. Carl guessed that only a few tens of thousands of people lived there, judging by its size. It was mid-morning by the time they'd got out of the spaceport and into the city. The streets were quiet.

Not many shuttles flew to Antarctica. They'd had to wait precious hours for the next available flight from London. Thankfully, Sayen didn't seem to have moved in all that time, according to the dot on the interface that showed the location of her tracker. Carl guessed that the Shadows must have decided to keep her in one place for the time being. That was what he hoped anyway. He didn't want to think about the other possible reason for her lack of movement.

"You trained here, didn't you?" Carl asked Harrington as they left the spaceport.

"Yep," Harrington replied.

"So, you must know the terrain pretty well."

"Yeah."

"And the conditions."

"That's right."

Carl waited for her to continue, but she didn't. Harrington had never been much of a talker, but Carl wondered about this especially silent streak she seemed to be going through.

The security officer pointed. "We can get vehicles over there."

Antarctica was the coldest place Carl had ever been. He pulled out a second jacket from his bag and put it on over the first as they walked over to the vehicle rental place.

When they got there, Harrington picked out three snowmobiles. The vehicles came equipped with snow goggles, thick mittens, and snowshoes. An assistant loaded the snowmobiles into a pickup truck and drove them to the edge of town. After Carl and Makey practiced driving the machines, the three of them set off across the flat, icy landscape.

On the horizon all around, the dirty white of the land melted into the cloudy sky, so that it wasn't possible to tell where one began and the other ended.

When McMurdo Sound was no longer visible behind them, Harrington stopped. Carl and Makey parked their vehicles beside her.

Carl got out the interface that showed Sayen's location. Harrington looked over his shoulder.

"It's that way," she said, nodding at a part of the landscape that looked no different from the rest. "As I see it, the place she's in has to be crawling with Shadows. There's no way we can take them all on. The best we can do is go inside, grab Sayen, and get out as fast as we can."

"Right," said Carl. "How do we do that?"

Harrington opened the bag of illegal stuff she'd bought

from the dero. "This might help." She got out a couple of large aerosol cans.

"We're gonna freshen them up until they disappear?" Carl asked.

"No," Harrington replied, straight-faced, "*we're* the ones who are going to disappear."

"That stuff will make us invisible?" Makey asked.

"Not exactly. It bends light. Anyone who's looking at something sprayed with this will see what's behind the object, unless they're at very close quarters. Whatever you spray it on isn't exactly invisible, but unless it moves, you probably won't notice it. In this landscape we have an advantage because it's harder to see things anyway. We lose that advantage when we go inside."

"So the Shadows won't see us unless we move?" asked Makey.

"That's right."

"I think we're gonna need to move to rescue your friend."

"Yes, we will, but you don't have to worry about that," Harrington said. "I want you to wait outside." She continued over his protests, "We need someone waiting to take Sayen back to the snowmobiles if Lingiari and I get caught. We don't want our effort to be wasted. We'll be relying on you, kid, in case something goes wrong."

"But I can help on the inside too," he said. "I want to help."

"Harrington's right," said Carl. "The more of us go in, the bigger the chance is of one of us being spotted. You've gotta think about the whole picture."

Makey nodded reluctantly.

"Good," said Harrington. "Now, let's spray ourselves before we get any closer to the place. We need to go on foot from here. We could spray the snowmobiles too, but they would hear them, so there's no point."

"So that stuff's illegal?" Carl asked. "Is it used by the military?"

"No, it isn't even available for restricted use," Harrington replied. "There are a few reasons, I think. One is because it contains a tiny amount of mythranil, which is banned of course. Another reason is because the substance failed safety tests. It causes psychological effects, probably due to the mythranil. Some test subjects developed psychoses.

"And I think the Government might also have banned it because of the havoc it would cause if it got into the general public's hands. Imagine the crimes people could commit if they could turn invisible."

"Hold on. So what you're saying is, this could make us insane?" Carl asked.

"It's a very slight possibility," Harrington said. "Are you ready?" She held up the can.

"Er...I suppose so."

"Lift up your arms and spread your legs. Hold your breath for as long as you can while it dries."

Carl did as she said. He heard a hissing sound, and tiny droplets of the invisibility spray landed on his skin, which tingled unpleasantly. He fought an urge to touch his face. Harrington's footsteps crunched on the ice as she walked around him. He heard the hissing sound again as she sprayed the back of his body.

"You ready, Makey?" she asked.

After a little while, when Carl's lungs were bursting, he exhaled. Harrington was finishing up spraying the kid. A very vague shape the same color as the landscape stood where Makey had been. If Carl hadn't been looking directly at him, he wouldn't have known he was there.

"My turn," said Harrington, holding out the can.

He began spraying her. Harrington's face and hair seemed to melt away into the pale gray ice behind her. Her shoulders and torso disappeared, and then her hips and legs. It was easy to spot any patches that he missed because they remained suspended in mid-air.

He turned to look for Makey.

"I'm here," Makey said.

The kid had moved. His voice came from somewhere to the right of where he'd been standing.

"Right," Harrington said. "If you want to show where you are, lift your snow goggles. We can't spray our eyes, so it's a good thing we're wearing them or we'd have to keep our eyes closed to slits to avoid being seen."

The woman's almond-shaped, deep reddish-brown eyes, eyebrows and a small portion of her face appeared briefly as she removed her goggles to demonstrate. They quickly disappeared into the landscape. When she moved, she was visible, but only vaguely, as if Carl were seeing her through a screen.

"Woah, what's that?" Makey asked. "What's happening?"

Carl felt it too. It was like he was floating in space. The landscape had become translucent and insubstantial. Then a moment later, he was in Antarctica again.

"It's the spray," Harrington said. "Try to ignore it. The effect wears off after a while. Let's go."

14

In the void, the Shadows waited.

Generation was proceeding at an acceptable pace on the planet called Earth. An early infiltration had occurred when the humans were unaware and unprepared. The process was always risky and vulnerable to failure in the beginning. Most often, the subjects would realize that one or two of their number had been replaced, and they would kill the ones who had replaced them before they had an opportunity to introduce more subjects to the traps.

But the initial invasion of Earth had succeeded before the humans had known what was happening. By then, it was too late. The quarantine they'd put in place after they understood the risk from their experiences on other planets had been doomed. The test they'd developed was effective, but the testers were mere humans. Replacing them had been easy.

Light years from Earth across the physical realm, on a trap planet, the most recent generation had nearly failed. Only one of their number had succeeded in deceiving the humans and surviving when their starship had crashed.

That one had arrived on Earth. Passing a test was simple when the tester was also one of them. That one from the trap planet had joined the generators.

They had replaced humans in many organizations that controlled Earth affairs, and their plan to introduce more subjects to the secret traps was succeeding. The moment was approaching when they would no longer have to hide, and large-scale generation could begin. Already, they had acquired many tracts of land in areas close to human habitation. At an appropriate time, traps would be activated in these places, and the humans could be replicated on a large scale. There were so many of this species, it would matter little if they destroyed those who resisted.

In these early stages, killing subjects was not desirable. It caused disturbance and confusion in the target population and raised suspicions. That problem had occurred in the area called Australia when two subjects had resisted. The effects of destroying those subjects were only just dying down.

Another impediment to the scheme had occurred when a human had succeeded in accessing information they held on the generation process. Attempts to replicate the human to prevent it from revealing the information had failed. The subject was not entirely organic, and the mechanism had faltered, as it always did with synthesized substances.

A further complication was that this human had a familial relationship with two others in positions of high influence. Replication was not possible, and yet they could not allow the subject to escape. If it alerted the population at large, all their plans could fail.

They could not allow that to happen. They needed more time to infiltrate and conquer the physical realm.

The Shadows debated the problem of the existence of

the part-synthetic human they had imprisoned. If replication was not possible, it seemed the only option was to destroy the subject. The effects would not be desirable, but perhaps they were unavoidable.

Replication. Generation. Domination. The plan had to succeed.

15

———

The air inside Sayen's metal box was getting colder and colder. The Shadows had taken her on another long flight, and she guessed she must be traveling south. She'd never known such low temperatures. Wearing only her underwear, she would have been suffering from hypothermia without her enhanced skin.

The Shadows hadn't been careful with her box as they'd loaded her onto the heli, and they were the same when they unloaded her. She was thrown from side to side, and at one point the box was upended, and what had been the ceiling became the floor. Sayen was desperately thirsty and hungry. For most of the flight she'd drifted in and out of consciousness.

Lying curled into a ball, Sayen wondered what the hell she'd been thinking of when she'd decided she wanted to finally live her life and not be overly cautious anymore. She wished she'd listened to her mother when she'd begged her to stay home, safe and secure. After nearly dying aboard the *Galathea*, she'd been crazy to put herself in danger again. She should let people like Jas and Carl handle the Shadows. She wasn't cut out to be a hero.

As she lay unmoving, Sayen tried to figure out why she hadn't been replicated. She was sure that had been the Shadows' intention, but something must have gone wrong. She wondered if it was something to do with her enhanced body. Maybe Shadows couldn't replicate synthetic materials, and so the cloning process wouldn't work.

The box had been still for so long, she began to wonder if the Shadows were going to leave her there forever. It wouldn't be a good way to die, but she couldn't get out, no matter how hard she tried. She had bloody bruises on her arms and legs to prove it.

A scraping sound came from outside. Something was being dragged across the metal. Sayen heard the rattle of chains falling, and at last the box opened.

She didn't recognize the expressionless faces of the four Shadows that stared in. These were different from the ones at the last place. All of them were pointing weapons at her.

"If you try to run or fight us, we will kill you," one of the female ones said.

Sayen reflected that they were probably going to kill her anyway, but she decided to play along for now. Grimacing with pain, she crawled out of the box and unsteadily stood up. They were inside a windowless room. It looked like some kind of classroom. She was inside a building, not a Shadow trap. The room was square and empty.

"Come with us," said the Shadow who had spoken. The four of them formed a guard around her, two in front, two behind, and together they went through the door. As they moved along, more Shadows passed them. Sayen's guard didn't speak to the others or even look at them. They passed ten or twelve Shadows.

Sayen was dismayed. They'd been going about five minutes, and the building seemed quite big. If it was full of Shadows, that meant there were already many of them on Earth.

How had the aliens gotten there?

A door opened as they arrived outside it, as if whoever opened it was aware of Sayen and her escort without seeing them. They went through, and Sayen found herself in something resembling a medical center. She shivered. At the best of times, she hated these places with their invasive machines. Then she caught sight of something that made her blood run cold. Half-hidden behind a large scanner was a long metal table fitted with restraints. A trough ran around the edges, leading to a pipe that disappeared into the floor. It was an autopsy table.

"Lie down," commanded the female Shadow, indicating the narrow bed that protruded from the scanner.

"Why?" Sayen croaked. "What are you going to do to me?"

A moment's silence passed. Carl had said he thought the Shadows were telepathic, and now Sayen was sure of it. They never spoke to each other, yet they seemed to know what the others were going to do before they acted.

A male Shadow shrugged, as if he thought the decision they had come to was unimportant. "We are going to investigate your physical body. We want to know why we could not replicate you, and we want to better understand the human form. We have attempted to do this investigation on ourselves as replicants of humans, but the process is uncomfortable and causes injuries. Human bodies also heal too slowly. We have no use for you because your body will not replicate, so we will take this opportunity to increase our knowledge."

Sayen thought she was going to faint. Her first impulse was to run, but she knew she wouldn't get far without being stunned again and brought back. Her stomach turned at the thought of waking up while being operated on by one of these creatures.

She had to take them all out at once to have a chance of escaping, and she would have to attack quickly to prevent them from communicating telepathically with others in the building.

Could she do it? All her attempts so far to escape had failed. Having an enhanced body wasn't enough. You also needed the skills and knowledge of how to use it. Sayen had been smart all her life. Why couldn't she find a way out of her predicament?

She swallowed. First, she needed time to think. "What...what's this machine?" she asked, indicating the scanner. "What does it do?"

"This machine allows us to see your internal structures and gives us information on how they work in unison. Readings taken while you are alive are the most useful to us. We will perform the invasive procedures last."

Legs trembling, Sayen lay down on the bed. A scan wouldn't harm her, and she still had no idea how she was going to get out of the situation. She wished she had Jas with her. Jas would know what to do. Jas would protect her.

The narrow bed was activated, and Sayen slid inside the machine. Whirrs and clicks started up, and her mind whirred too.

Four of them have weapons. Four weapons is a lot, but I only need to get one and kill them all before they have a chance to shoot me. She grimaced. *Yeah, that's all, Sayen. How're you going to do it?*

Too soon, the machine stopped and the bed she was

lying on slid out of it. Three Shadows stood around her and two were looking at a screen. Of the ones standing near, only one had its weapon trained on her. The others had returned theirs to holsters around their waists. Sayen estimated it would take them at least a second—maybe longer—to draw and fire.

But the moment she reached for the weapon pointing at her, the Shadow holding it would shoot, and it would be all over for her. She was sure the Shadows wouldn't mind giving up on their scientific investigations and killing her if they thought she was a risk to them. Though she was shaking with fear, she would have to keep her cool and wait for the right moment.

"Sit up," said the man.

One of the Shadows at the screen came over to her, holding an ophthalmoscope. They must have noticed her enhanced eyes on the scan. The Shadow held up the instrument in its hand to Sayen's face and leaned toward it to read the display panel on the back.

Sayen blinked slowly, twice, to activate her enhancement. Her eyes zoomed in on the skin of the Shadow's face, and Sayen could see it in minute detail—the fine hairs sprouting from pores, the tiny sweat glands, the ridges and furrows, even a miniscule, blind mite. She shuddered. Shadows really were physically identical to the humans they replaced.

Who had this Shadow replaced? What had been her job? Had she been married? Had she had a family? To create the five Shadows in the room, five people had died. Sayen thought of Carl's missing parents, and wondered how many people the Shadows had killed. How many more would kill they if they weren't stopped?

She thought of her parents being replaced by these evil

aliens. Her fear began to give way to rage. If she didn't make it home, it would break her parents' hearts. She wasn't going to let that happen.

She was furious at these *things* that had trapped her.

"Your eyes are partly synthetic," said the Shadow. "Their capabilities exceed the limits of natural human eyes. Do many humans have modifications like yours?"

"Yes," Sayen spat. "Lots of us have. That's why you couldn't replicate me, and why you won't be able to replicate them. And the enhancements I have are nothing compared to most of theirs. They'll *kill* you."

The Shadow moved its gaze from the display screen to look directly into Sayen's eyes. "I think you're lying. We have replicated many humans. You are the first that we couldn't replicate."

Sayen locked eyes with the creature for a moment, until it broke under her stare and turned away.

Another Shadow approached with an otoscope. They'd noticed her enhanced hearing during her scan, too. As the creature examined her ears, she watched the others in the room, noting their positions and their level of attention to her. They were paying her less mind than at first.

"We want you to run on this," one of them said, pointing to a treadmill. Sayen went over to the machine, and the Shadow attached a mask to her face to measure her respiration. It turned on the machine, and kept a weapon trained on her while it adjusted the controls.

Sayen walked on the treadmill, then jogged, then ran, as the machine sped up. All the while, the Shadow looked from her to the machine's display and back to her. In the rest of the room, Sayen could see three of the other Shadows, but she didn't know where the final one was.

She was lucky. The Shadow she couldn't see was the one

that didn't have a weapon. She couldn't risk looking around to find where it was, or she might alert the Shadow watching her as to her intentions. She would just have to take a chance that she would locate the unseen Shadow before it could react.

The Shadow by the treadmill continued to watch. Its gaze flitted to her again. Then to the treadmill display. To her. She was sprinting now, faster than humanly possible. But with her enhanced body, she was barely panting. Her eyes were locked on the Shadow's.

To her. To the display. To her. To the—

Sayen pushed off with her right foot. She overtook the speed of the treadmill. Leaping over the front of it, she grabbed the Shadow's weapon and kicked it down. Its head cracked on the floor, but Sayen didn't see the impact. As it was falling, she was already turning and firing. One Shadow fell with a scream, a red, smoking hole in its chest. Another raised its hands in self-defense as the aim of Sayen's weapon traveled toward its face, but the beam sliced through its palms. A larger cavity opened where its mouth had been.

Sayen spun round. The third Shadow had made it to the door and was opening it. She got it in the back before it could take a step outside.

Where was the fourth? She had to stop it from broad-casting to the others. She scanned the room, but there was no sign of the creature. There was only one possible place it could hide.

She went to the corner of the room and looked under the autopsy bed. The Shadow's eyes met hers. She saw fear in them. Sayen hesitated for a split second. Then she remembered the woman whose life the Shadow had taken.

Her jaw firmed. She raised the weapon and fired.

16

———

They must have walked two or three miles in their snowshoes, Carl estimated. His nose, fingers, and toes were numb from the cold, in spite of the exertion, and his face smarted from the steady, chill wind. His mind was also spinning from the effects of the invisibility spray. One moment he was on solid ground, the next it seemed like he was stepping into eternal nothingness.

Keeping track of the other two was also hard. Every few minutes they would all speak to indicate their location and move closer if they'd drifted too far apart.

Harrington had coated three weapons with the invisibility spray and handed one each to Carl and Makey, emphasizing that they had to take special care to know what they were shooting at to avoid shooting each other. She'd also pointed out that if they dropped their weapon, it was as good as lost.

Though she'd sprayed the bag of equipment she was carrying, she hadn't treated anything else inside it. Every so often, the interface that showed Sayen's location would appear mysteriously in mid-air and float around for a few moments before disappearing into nothingness again.

After one of these appearances, Carl heard Harrington mumble to herself.

"Shouldn't we be getting close?" he asked.

"Yes, we should," she replied. "According to the readings, Sayen's being held only two or three hundred meters from here."

The landscape in front of them remained bare and empty of life.

"Do you think the readings are wrong?" he asked.

"No, I don't think so."

"Then where is she?"

"I've been thinking about it. The Shadows are operating in secret for the moment. Any place where they congregate has to be hidden to avoid causing suspicion. I think Sayen's right where this thing says she is. Except she's underground."

"The Shadows have an underground base here?" asked Makey.

"I spent a few years living here," Harrington replied. "There are research facilities all over the place. It wouldn't surprise me if one of the old superpowers built a secret underground facility. If the Shadows occupied one, it would be the perfect hiding place for them."

"Krat," Carl said. "How are we going to get inside?"

"We'll figure out a way," Harrington replied. "Makey, this is where you wait. You remember what Sayen looks like from seeing her on the *Galathea*, right? She looks the same now, just conscious. If you see her, go to her and help her back to the snowmobiles."

"But—"

"Makey, that's an order. If you want to work in security, you'd better learn to follow them."

Carl heard an adolescent huff come from Makey's direction.

"Let's get going, Jas," he said. It had been many hours since they'd first learned of Sayen's disappearance. Every moment they delayed could mean the difference between success and failure.

"Just a second." A roll of thin rope appeared from the security officer's bag. She put it on the ground. "This is our rendezvous. It's not great, but it's better than nothing. Makey, stay here until you see Sayen, in case we need to find you."

CARL AND JAS went the final distance together. They talked as quietly as the low whistle of the wind would allow.

"How are we going to get in?" Carl asked.

"The entrance has to be disguised to look the same as the surroundings, or we'd see it by now. But the Shadows have human bodies. In this environment, they need heat, and heat will escape through any gap."

A pair of binoculars appeared from thin air and floated over to Carl.

"What do you see?"

Carl held the binoculars up to his eyes, and the landscape was transformed to grey shapes beneath a glowing sky. Except in one place. Four bright lines formed a square only a few meters from where they stood.

"We're right on top of them," he said. He removed the binoculars and focused his gaze on the spot that had shown the heat signature. As he went nearer, the faint lines marking the edges of a hatch became visible. "Over here." Now that he looked closely at it, the ice over the hatch didn't glisten like the rest. It was artificial, but without looking directly at it, he would never have been able to tell.

He felt something swipe him. It was Harrington's hand. She grabbed his arm.

"Great," she said. "I can see it too. According to the tracer, Sayen's about twenty meters farther on in the same direction." She sighed. "I was hoping we wouldn't have to do it this way. If we could kill a guard and slip in, we'd have a little time before they realized what was happening. But we don't have an alternative. We'll have to surprise them and rely on chaos and confusion."

"What do you mean?"

"I'm going to blow the door in."

The bag rustled.

"This has a two-minute fuse," Harrington said as an explosive device appeared. "The second it blows, we go in. After that...krat. I don't know. I don't know what we'll find in there—how big the place is, or how many Shadows there are. We're going to lose each other the minute we're inside, and we won't be able to talk or we'll give ourselves away. I guess we just have to find her, get out, and get back to Makey. Whatever happens, don't wait for me. Go to the snowmobiles. I can find my own way back."

"The same for me," said Carl. There didn't seem much more for either to say.

They withdrew to a safe distance.

"Cover your ears," Harrington said, just before the explosive blew. As a gaping hole appeared in the ice, Carl was already running toward it. He leapt in and straight down into the Shadows' base. The door had ripped the hand bars from the wall before embedding into the floor.

Carl landed on it and moved quickly away. As he expected, he heard a thunk as Harrington jumped down behind him.

Smoke from the explosion filled the air. Carl headed in the only direction that was clear. Shadows were already approaching the scene of the explosion. He slipped past them easily and went deeper into the base.

As he ran, he wondered what he was looking for. Where would the Shadows keep their prisoners? Sayen could be anywhere. Harrington had been right. The place did seem to be a research facility. He'd already passed several labs. A chill sweat broke out on him. Had the Shadows brought Sayen there because they wanted to experiment on her?

He was heading into an area of classrooms. He doubled back to return to the research laboratories, though he dreaded what he might find.

A Shadow ran out of a doorway, and Carl crashed into it. The creature landed heavily and stared around in confusion. Carl jumped over the Shadow and sped away, wondering at what he had seen. For a moment, Carl had experienced the drifting into nothingness that was an effect of the invisibility spray. At that moment, he'd looked at the Shadow, and seen a faint light around the man, like sunspots on his retinas on a sunny day. He ran on.

No shout or cry came from behind him, but if the Shadows were telepathic as he suspected, the information about invisible assailants was probably being broadcast.

He had to find Sayen fast.

The Shadow base was eerily silent. No alarms were ringing due to the explosion at the door. No one was shouting commands. But Carl could hear something else. It sounded like a fight was going on. He could hear grunts, gasps, and the sound of bodies hitting the floor.

As he turned a corner, he came upon a strange sight.

Four Shadows were wrestling with an invisible opponent. Carl got a glimpse of a pair of beautiful, reddish-brown eyes. Harrington's snow goggles had come off and the Shadows had caught her. If he didn't do something soon, they would hold her still enough to get in a shot.

He aimed to fire, but he risked hitting Harrington. The disorientation effect of the invisibility spray hit him again. The Shadows before him glowed faintly. He blinked, and the glow was gone.

He had to concentrate. He would have to take them out close up. Before he could move, Sayen appeared, running toward them from the opposite direction. She was in her underwear, and she was a mess—covered in bruises, scratches, and dried blood. But she was alive. Now he just had to save Harrington and get Sayen out.

The woman's eyebrows rose at the sight of the struggling Shadows, and she slowed her pace.

"It's Harrington," Carl called. "They've got her. Get out of the way. I'm going to shoot."

Sayen looked in his direction, her face brightening in recognition of his voice. She slowed to a stop. The Shadows, on hearing him speak, loosened their grip on Harrington. They also noticed Sayen.

She had a weapon in her hand. She raised it and shot one of the Shadows in the stomach. As it fell to the floor, another was thrown head first into the wall by an unseen force. Carl shot a third, which was coming in his direction, trying to find the source of the words he'd spoken. The fourth aimed at Sayen, but the beam from her weapon cleaved its skull.

"Carl, Jas, where are you?" Sayen said.

Carl ran to her and grabbed her. "I'm here. Let's go. The exit's this way. Harrington, are you behind us?"

"Yes, I'm coming. Go."

Gripping Sayen's arm, Carl ran with her back to the blown-in door. When they reached it, they had a problem. With the hand bars ripped off, the hole was too high to reach. Then Carl had an idea.

"Climb on my shoulders, and I'll lift you up."

"Where are you?"

"Here." He put her hands on his shoulders and squatted down. When Sayen was aboard, he rose to his feet. Sayen was in reach of the edge of the hatchway. He felt her stand on his shoulders to scramble out. He'd done it. They'd saved her.

"Makey's due east, Sayen. He's waiting for you, and he'll take you to McMurdo Sound."

"Krat that, Carl, I'm not leaving without you." She was leaning over the hatch looking down at him.

"You'll have to. I can't make it up there."

"I might not be able to see you, but I can pull you up."

"You can't. I'm too heavy."

"You really think so? Try me." She gave two small grunts. "I've anchored my feet in the ice. Grab my hands."

Carl jumped and gripped the woman's small hands. He swung there for a moment, then, unbelievably, he found himself being lifted upward and out of the Shadow base.

The moment he could reach the edge of the hatchway with his knee, he levered himself the rest of the way. Sayen was grinning.

Now they just had to get Harrington. He looked into the hatch and quickly drew his head away as Shadows in the corridor fired at him. He caught a brief glimpse of return fire from Harrington below him. She was using the door as cover.

"Harrington," he shouted down.

"I've set a bomb," came her voice directly below him. "Run. Get Sayen away."

But the woman was scrabbling back to the hole. "Jas, take my hands." She thrust her arms into the hatch, and screamed. Her face was twisted in pain, but she heaved an invisible Harrington out of the hole.

They ran.

The ground shuddered, and Carl was thrown down as the Shadow base exploded behind him. Smoking debris began to rain from the sky. He scrambled to his feet, and went to continue, but the body of a Shadow fell in front of him. Carl halted in horror. The thing was still alive. It had a weapon in its hand. It was aiming at Carl. Rooted to the spot, there was nothing he could do.

Then the weapon sailed out of the Shadow's hand. Someone had kicked it away. Harrington?

The Shadow died.

17

"That's it, Makey," Harrington said through her teeth. "When we get back to London, you're on your own. No more mentoring. You're not fit to work in security or anywhere else where people put their lives in your hands."

The security officer was somewhere off to Carl's right. They were nearly back at the snowmobiles. He could see them a short distance away, black against the pale gray ice.

Harrington's words were the first she'd spoken since they'd left the remains of the Shadow base. Her pitch was low and calm, but it was clear she was in an absolute rage.

"What? Why?" came the kid's voice from his left.

"I gave you a direct order to stay by the rope. You disobeyed. You followed us to the Shadow base. If there's one thing you must never, ever do, it's disobey an order."

"Come on, Harrington," Carl said. "He saved my life when he kicked that Shadow's weapon away."

"That's how it looked to me, too," added Sayen. She was still wearing very little clothing, and she was walking barefoot across the ice, but she'd assured them that she was fine.

She'd explained that the body enhancements that had enabled her to lift both Carl and Harrington out of the Shadow base also protected her from extreme heat and cold.

Across her forearms, however, the skin was burned and blistered where the beam from a Shadow's weapon had scored it when she'd reached into the hole for a second time. Without her enhanced skin, her arms would have been severed.

"Don't interfere with things you don't understand, Carl," Jas said. "You were lucky, kid, that's all. You could have died, or you could have gotten the rest of us killed. You never disobey an order. If you don't get that, it's over. Forget it."

Carl said, "Jas, don't you—"

"This is none of your business," she exclaimed.

Anger rose in Carl in return. The woman's temper got on his nerves, and in this case it wasn't justified. Makey was just a kid, and he'd been a big help at a sticky moment. But before Carl could reply, Harrington continued, "When we get back to the snowmobiles, we need to change our clothes and wipe off the spray. Then we head straight to the spaceport. There are probably Shadows in McMurdo Sound, and I don't know how long we have before they're alerted about us."

The invisibility spray came off when scrubbed with handfuls of ice. By the time he was free of the sticky substance, Carl was freezing. His hands were red and raw from holding the ice, and he could barely feel them. He thrust them into his mittens, but that made little difference. It was odd seeing Makey and Jas slowly reappear as they cleaned off the spray. Sayen stood by, her arms wrapped around herself, watching them all in amusement.

"How are we going to get Sayen on a shuttle?" Makey asked. "She doesn't have any ID."

"Don't worry," Sayen said. "I don't think it'll be a problem. But I do need some clothes. I don't suppose you have any to spare?"

Makey was the closest in size of the three of them to the petite woman, but she still looked ridiculous in his pants, rolled up at the ankles, and his sweater, which hung almost to her knees.

They decided they couldn't risk taking the time to get her anything more suitable. They had to get out of McMurdo Sound before the Shadows made a move against them.

Before they set off, Harrington mailed a one-word message to Sayen's parents: Success.

Jas was silent all the way to the spaceport, and Carl didn't say much either. He remained angry with her over her tirade at Makey. He was beginning to wonder what he'd ever seen in her. She could be moody and difficult, and her outbursts of temper were annoying.

Harrington's message seemed to have born fruit when they arrived at the check in for the next flight to the U.S. The clerk didn't ask to see any of their IDs, and neither did the shuttle staff when they boarded.

Carl, Sayen, and Makey sat three abreast, while Harrington sat across from them. From the look on her face, Carl would never have guessed that they had just saved their friend from grave danger and taken out twenty or thirty Shadows. He didn't know if he would ever figure her out, and he wasn't sure if he wanted to try. He turned to Sayen.

"So, what did you find out that made them come for

you?" he asked in a low voice, taking care not to be overheard in the public passenger cabin.

"I'll explain later," she replied. "But one thing I can say is, they're good at mimicking us. I thought my manager was a sweet man, but it turned out he was one of them. We can't trust anyone."

Carl thought of his parents. Would he ever find them? And if he did, could he be sure it was really them?

Across the aisle, Harrington's interface beeped. She swiped the screen to read the message. Her sour expression turned sourer still. Wordlessly, she handed the screen across to Sayen. As she read it, the woman's face fell.

She angled the device so that Carl and Makey could also see it.

Please do not bring our daughter home. We're so sorry. They know who you are. It's no longer safe to come here. You must disappear. Don't use anything that will allow you to be traced. A friend will meet you at the spaceport you're traveling to and give you a package. Good luck. S, we love you, darling.

Sayen looked like she was about to cry. Carl put an arm over her shoulders.

"Don't worry. We defeated them back there, like we did aboard the *Galathea*. They're not invincible. We'll find out who they are, and we'll destroy them. Whether they're in government, or corporations, or the military, or even if they've made it to the Transgalactic Council itself. We'll get them all. They aren't going to win."

JAS'S STORY CONTINUES IN
UNDERWORLD

SHADOWS OF THE VOID BOOK 5

Sign up to my reader group for a free copy of *Starbound*, the Shadows of the Void prequel that tells the story of what happened to Jas Harrington in Antarctica, and for discounts on new releases, advanced reader opportunities and other interesting stuff:

https://jjgreenauthor.com/free-books/

(I won't send spam or pass on your details to a third party.)